WANDERERS OF THE FIELD

This is a novel about migrant farm workers. All of his life Jack O'Neal has known the joy of moving from one place to another, winter and summer, spring and fall, following the crops with his family. Jack is a hard-working boy, and when his father suddenly dies he shoulders the responsibility for supporting himself, his mother, and his little sister. In addition, he takes upon himself the burden of repaying a loan old Colonel House, a plantation owner, had made to Jack's father.

Picking, grubbing, and clearing is back-breaking labor for them all, but there is fun and adventure too as they move through the South in the old truck that serves as their home. And they meet all sorts of interesting people, the kind stay-at-homes never get to know.

In the end something good happens to Jack, and he knows that thereafter his mother and sister will not have to work the fields again. But not before the reader has had a rare opportunity to get to know the life of the wanderers of the field.

WANDERERS
OF THE FIELD

A NOVEL BY

George Harmon Smith

The John Day Company
New York

WANDERERS OF THE FIELD

Chapter 1

In predawn's gray light Jack O'Neal saw the nanny goat. She grazed along the crest of the levee, the rusty bell on the leather strap around her neck clapping the virgin, pristine air with faint dingdongs as she stepped.

"Nanny Bell! Nanny Bell! Now you come on here!" he shouted.

There was a guttural snarl in the marsh grass below the levee, beyond the place where the truck was parked, and then Jack saw Roosevelt, his eager tawny-colored male boxer, with his ears standing at attention like two alert sentinels—saw the warm eyes set in the churn-sized head, heard the hissing snarl of Roosevelt's big feet in the dry leaves as he came bounding up the gradual slope to where Jack stood, now his belly flattening against the black earth, making those haunting sounds of love deep in his throat. A warm wet tongue flicked out against Jack's hand, then the huge dog, in a frenzy of love, began to buck and rear and leap against Jack's slight body, pushing him off balance.

7

Jack shouted him down, and as he lay there quivering in the fecund earth, his eyes like black agate marbles, Jack turned and pointed at the nanny goat.

"Fetch, boy!" he commanded.

Roosevelt stood up. He cocked his head inquisitively, his stump of tail going like a metronome set for a hot electric guitar.

"Fetch Nanny Bell!" Jack said again. "But don't hurt her—just bring her home."

With a joyful cry, Roosevelt was off like a brown telegram, humping his rippling back as he climbed the Mississippi River levee, in the gentle crook it made below Lake Providence, cutting across the canal the Federal troops had dug during the siege of Vicksburg.

Once Nanny Bell saw the huge boxer bearing down on her, she reared up on her hind legs, let out a frightened baaaaaaaa, then came leaping down through the dry grass, the bell jingling fitfully, all the way to where the truck was parked, with Roosevelt nipping at her heels.

From the tent behind the truck there came an angry shout, then Jack saw Mama O'Neal rush out from behind the truck bed, brandishing a worn-out broom; saw her set in on Roosevelt, whacking him lustily about the head; saw the way Nanny Bell cowed down behind Mama O'Neal, her head low and trembling visibly. But Roosevelt, who'd long been jealous of the goat, which had been bought that first summer when Papa O'Neal had come down with an ulcerated stomach, stubbornly circled the frightened Nanny, barking and snarling.

Somehow, it tickled Jack, the way Mama O'Neal was lunging out at the dog, her skirts popping about her meaty legs, the stiff finger (the index finger, the one the old sow had crushed) standing up like a mailbox flag.

Mama heard Jack's laughter, whirled around, and waved the broom angrily.

"Call off that beast!" she shouted. "Jack O'Neal, ain't you got a lick of sense!"

He began to shout the boxer down, and on hearing his master's voice, Roosevelt backed off some, turned and gazed at him a moment, then went blukety-blukety up the levee, until he came up to Jack, then leaped into his arms, his tongue flicking out like a hot, wet dagger against his cheek.

Mama O'Neal turned to comfort the frightened goat, her words like honey bubbles, and as Nanny Bell gloried in this bit of attention, baaaaaaing appreciatively, she turned on Jack again.

"A *body* just don't know her own son!" she shouted. "Jack O'Neal, you knowed better than to set that beast on our only source of milk! Lord, Wesley ain't been passed away but a week now, and you've already started making me trouble! A body would think you'd have better sense than to scare the all-fired heck out of our purty little goat, who gives the only food we can count on for sure."

"Mama, she wouldn't come in!" he said, pointedly.

9

"Well, that was no cause to set the dog on her! Why, I bet she's so scared, she don't give down her milk for two days!"

"Ah, Mama."

That was all he ever said. You couldn't reason with her. He'd discovered that long ago. So he climbed the levee until her words were unclear, until she was lost from his view, and he was then standing at the crest of the levee, looking out at the silent yellow-backed Father of Waters. Around the bend there came a hoarse hoot, and he saw the blue snuffing of burnt diesel fuel and the line of flatboats being pushed up the river.

For a moment Jack stood there listening to the muted honk honk of the air horn, and then he turned and stared across the endless Delta stretching away into blurred heat waves and dancing dots to the west, greener where the young cotton plants were growing, and light gray where the land was fallow. The view sent a warm empty feeling through him, and let memory into his mind—memory he had been trying to push back for two days; memory that had kept him awake last night.

The memory that his father was dead!

It was so unreal, all of it. That wasn't his father's humped grave over there in the Truxno Graveyard. Why, any minute now he would hear the early morning sounds of him—his gum-rubber boots going suck-ah suck-ah in the dew-wet grass beyond the tent, the song he sang, as he went about the job of milking Nanny Bell, before going to the cotton field.

"I've gambled down in Washington, I've gambled down in Spain, I'm going back to Florida, to gamble my last game.
Oh, Mother, dear Mother, you know I love you well,
But the love I have for that gambling man no human tongue can tell."

Funny that a field tramp who'd never gambled on anything risking money, would pick a song like that, Jack thought. But that had been his father's song. Jack had heard it in the truck farm country of northern Florida, in the delta flats of Mississippi, Louisiana, and Arkansas; in the hot tomato patches of central Arkansas, in the cool, mountainous apple orchards of western Arkansas, southern Missouri and eastern Oklahoma; in the hot, dry cotton fields on the high plains of west Texas, in the trucker's muck of the Rio Grande Valley.

"I've been eating too much fried stuff lately," his father had said, only last week when they'd been chopping cotton on Sandyland Plantation, just across the river from Lake Providence, on the Mississippi side. "My old ulcers are kicking up their heels again . . . got to stick to my goat milk."

But he just couldn't withstand the temptation of

11

fatback, fried in a black skillet, with potatoes soggy-fried in the same grease. Each day he had chopped cotton in the hot sun until his jeans and blue jumper were wet and salt-rimed, then come home at night and complained about the pain in his belly.

Three nights ago it was, Jack had been awakened by the shrill cries of his mother: "Come here, son! Come here!"

But even when he came to the cot in the little tent and saw the crimson oozing out of his father's mouth, he knew it was too late. The face was already cold, clammy; the eyes rolled upward, exposing the whites. There was a puddle of blood with black clots the size of green walnuts in it on one side of the cot near his father's sweat-stiffened jeans; an empty medicine box, with the cotton packing lying beside it, near the folding chair.

"Run, Jack, run!" Mama O'Neal had cried. "Tell Colonel House! Tell him, git the doctor quick!"

Jack had run toward the great, columned antebellum mansion with the upstairs windows seen like socketless eyes on moonlit nights; had roused up the old Colonel, who'd called Dr. Rudley; but when the eccentric country practitioner had arrived at the O'Neal tent, Wesley was breathing like he'd just run home from the field ahead of a mad fox. He'd bled down to water.

For a time, as he waited outside the entrance of the tent, Jack had heard Dr. Rudley's tense voice speaking to his mother, the muffled sounds of the opening and closing of his big black bag, and then there had been a strange stillness inside the tent. Jack remembered how the katydids were fiddling in the dead grass back toward the pasture where the barb-wire fence snaked; remembered the little wind that came from nowhere and whispered in the ragged tent flaps. Then, in a weak, unclear voice his father had called for his family, as though he knew he was dying.

Mama O'Neal had come for Jack. "He's asking for you, son," she choked out. "You better hurry!"

Jack had taken the cold hand just after Peggy Jo had left the tent bawling; had heard the faint, hoarse words, like it was that time last winter when his father had a sore throat and nearly lost his voice.

"Son?"

"Yes, Dad."

"You're the man now . . . ain't taught you much, fiddlefooting all over the country . . . got to see after your mama and sister . . . you all they got."

"I—I will, Dad!" Jack was ashamed of the girlish squeak of his voice. He tried to clear his throat, but the lump wouldn't come up or go down.

Did the fingers of that great work-enlarged hand tighten on his small one? Was that a poor make-out-of-a-smile on his father's lips? He didn't know for sure. And then Dr. Rudley was gently pulling him aside, was kneeling beside the cot.

Jack stood with his mother near the entrance. On the sagging, bloody cot in one corner of the tent, the body of Wesley O'Neal lay, the face looking wan, as white as cotton, and tired . . . tired . . . but with a peace setting upon the sad corners of the thin mouth, silence slowly erasing away the lines of pain and hunger and living from hand to mouth, the eyelids fluttering, closing for the unbroken sleep. Wesley O'Neal would labor no more in the Deep South sun.

Jack stood looking—looking to Mama O'Neal who choked back her sobs and tiptoed out; and to Peggy Jo who tiptoed in, stood still, looking, cried her tears of want and longing, whispered, "Daddy, Daddy!" and backed up toward the entrance into the arms of her mother; and then he heard only the lulling singing of the katydids beyond the tent in the dead grass where the barb-wire fence snaked.

That night was when Jack learned about loneliness. He thought he knew all about it long before. In the schools he'd attended, he'd been too proud to force himself on his age group, his classmates, who looked on him as an outsider, so he'd played alone.

This was different; this was it—the yawning black hole of loneliness, and he had to look into it alone. Colonel House had given the coffin of gray; had seen to the preacher for the funeral, and since Mama O'Neal could not ask him to give money with which to send the body by hearse back to the red-clay hills of Georgia, the land of Wesley O'Neal's youth, the coffin was brought to the great, old house and carefully placed at one end of the seventy-by-thirty living room, and people who'd known his father came slowly up the steps, whispering and nodding—and many who'd never known him, yet respecting Colonel House.

Jack was lying on a pallet spread down on one end of the great porch, and the crowds that came did not see him. But he heard their whispers as they paused outside the door waiting their turn.

"It is a pity, ain't it, Dicey Mae?" came a woman's voice.

"Yes, it is . . . I mean, him leaving that poor little girl, and all, you know . . ."

"Yes, I do."

Jack lay still on the pallet, looking out at the moony night. Two of Colonel House's bird dogs, their claws silvery in the dewy grass, nervously sniffed the air and growled softly when the Mexicans, walking in football huddles, came past. And he'd smelled the Cape jasmine bushes in the side yard; the lingering scent of cigarette smoke.

If only some one of them would come to him and just touch his forehead . . . say something to him . . . even bawl him out!

But no one came; and no one knew of the sudden panic pounding of his heart, the smothering deadly loneliness. And the fear.

He heard some one of the women speak of the funeral. "It'll be a pauper's funeral," she'd whispered. "Don't you feel sorry for *her*, though . . . I mean, you know, Bessie . . ."

"Yes, Ruth."

15

For a long time he thought about the word, pauper, and wondered what it meant, exactly. And he thought he knew.

It was a time of too much, too many . . . too much of the wrong kind of talk; too many of the curious, who'd come there out of sick curiosity. And so he smelled the Cape jasmine bushes and the scent of them was that other part of being dead, for he smelled the scent again in Old Truxno Graveyard the next day, when he numbly followed the hearse through the rusted iron gate.

There were no close relatives, other than the immediate family; no darling aunt for him to lean upon; no hand to pat his shoulder, no voice that whispered comforting words. But many of the migratory choppers and wetbacks who'd known his father had come there to the funeral, walking carefully past the old, sunken graves, to the raw fresh earth hump with the artificial grass round about it.

The country preacher, Reverend Josiah Harper, in a shiny blue serge suit, had been found at the last moment, and he stumbled over the sermon in a singsong halting manner, like a mule trying to find his way across a cattle gap. But toward the end, even though the crowd was small, coarse, and some no more than curious, he found himself, and his words rang so forcefully in Jack's ears that he forgot the sickening scent of the Cape jasmine bushes, and that his father was dead, even . . . .

He spoke of a promised land, and his words were comforting. "Beyond this low ground of sin and sorrow is the place where Wesley O'Neal has gone, where there will be neither wars nor rumors of wars; neither sickness nor death, nor sorrow, nor want, nor fear, nor greed, nor lust, nor hatred; so wipe away thy tears, dear ones who mourn for him! He has gone to a far better place than this which thou knowest."

Jack took one last look at the strange set face, then he was going back the way he'd come, weeping silently into the evening stillness, hearing only the hushed drone of voices of those taking one last farewell, too.

Late yesterday afternoon he'd gone to the graveyard again. Already the white roses had wilted in the hot baked earth, and there were the shy footprints of a bunny where the earth was loose.

Later, he went back up the winding lane thinking of this man, his father, dead at forty-six, a fiddlefoot sacrifice, with memories of hopeless, endless days in the hot fields which had belonged to other men, and with the memories of blue wistful hills in the Ozarks when the apples flamed red and he and his father had followed a coon dog through October woods one frosty night.

Since all of the cotton had been chopped on Colonel House's plantation, many of the Spanish Americans, traveling in fifth-hand Buicks and beat-up flatbed trucks with tarps stretched over the frame behind the cab, had left Big D Plantation, going north toward Lake Village, and the Arkansas line.

Early that morning Jack had put on fresh jeans, a clean T-shirt, and had walked up to the old plantation manor, going to the front door, and as he knocked and the colored woman came, he wondered what Colonel House wanted.

"Colonel House sent for me," Jack said.

"Come in, take a chair," the woman invited in a high, shrill voice.

He entered the huge living room, but instead of sitting down in one of the leather-covered chairs, stood beside the marble-topped table looking out at the Colonel's side yard where bird dogs romped.

The maid came back for Jack and led him to the Colonel's office, opened the door, then closed it behind him. Jack stood in front of the Colonel's desk, his straw hat in one hand, a slight boy of sixteen with blue frightened eyes and a perfect blond face, except where the deep, black scar ran jaggedly from one corner of his left eye into his wide forehead. In school, whenever they'd stayed in one place long enough for him and Peggy Jo to attend, with one hand he'd subconsciously cover the scar, which had been the result of his having fallen against the black washpot when he was three years old.

Finally, Colonel House looked up from the desk. "Hello, Jack," he smiled. "I guess you're wondering why I sent for you?"

"Yes, sir."

"Well, let me show you."

18

He got up from his leather-covered armchair and went to a filing cabinet, produced a key, inserted it in the lock and opened the cabinet.

While his back was turned, Jack was able to see the room—the lacy curtains at the windows, the chrome-trimmed air conditioner in the window nearest the desk, the silver plate hung from the marble mantleboard, and the screen in front of the small fireplace, which would be left there until late fall.

Colonel House closed the metal drawer, came back to his desk holding some kind of paper in one rosy hand. He eased down and told Jack to sit down for a minute.

"How has your maw been making out?" Colonel House asked.

"All right, considering, but Peggy Jo is still crying a lot at night," Jack returned.

"Poor little lost rose!" And then, "I hate to show you this paper, but I paid for the—ah—funeral arrangements and as the saying goes, *biness* is *biness*."

He slid the paper across the desk. "This is a promissory note, son."

Jack looked at it; recognized his father's signature. "Yes, sir."

"You see, son, your father owed me two hundred and forty-seven dollars for getting the truck overhauled the last time."

"I didn't know that, sir," Jack said. "Why, that was way last winter, wasn't it?"

Jack wondered how his father had borrowed money from the Colonel with the family way off down in the Rio Grande Valley all winter.

"Well, the fact is, Jack, your dad wrote me a letter and asked for money, and since he'd been chopping and picking cotton on my land for so many years, I couldn't deny him."

"Well, sir, you should have held our last paycheck," Jack said, his face reddening. "It wasn't much, but it was your money."

"No, I don't do *biness* that way," Colonel House returned. And then, "It takes money to make money, son. Your dad had been paying me back in fives along. I thought that if you should do pretty well this summer and fall—well, ah . . . you could send me a little along, you know."

The Colonel made an impressive figure before the desk. He was a big man with a red face, and with long white hair above light blue eyes, which somehow reminded Jack of a friendly circus lion. On one rosy finger he wore a diamond ring as big as a buckeye ball.

"I'll do the best I can, sir," Jack promised. "But you know how high-priced canned goods are and—"

"Now, don't you go hungry, boy! Don't put yourself in a strain, but if you get *some* ahead, well just send it. If you don't, that's all right, too," Colonel House cut in.

"I'll pay it!"

Colonel House looked at Jack a long time, then said, "Well, son, you're sixteen. It won't hurt you to sweat, but I want you to think about something important. Don't stay on the road too long. What are you doing about your education?"

"I've gone to school when I could," Jack said sadly.

"And we live in an age, Jack, when you must go to school. Already, chemicals and cotton pickers are replacing migrants."

"I have my books. Mr. Jason—he was the principal of Delno High School—let me keep them."

"Study them at night, Jack."

"Yes, sir."

"Good luck, son."

"Thank you, Colonel House," Jack said, softly. "I sure wish I could promise you exactly when I will pay back the money, but I just don't know!"

"Don't worry about it. I like that answer better than an easy promise, Jack." The Colonel smiled.

He walked beside Jack to the door, his rosy hand on Jack's shoulder.

"Good luck!" he said, at the steps. And then, "If you should have bad luck, don't fail to let me hear from you."

Jack nodded, going quickly toward the gate.

Chapter 2

Jack cradled the steering wheel and craned his neck to see through the bug-splattered windshield, and with his tongue against his lips, tasted the late evening dust—black loam, cotton poisoning, and burnt gasoline.

"I reckon a body could go from here to tarnation and never get away from this cussed old Delta," Mama mused, her eyes scanning the gloomy fields.

"I've got the fantods," Peggy Jo whimpered. "When do we stop and eat?"

All three were riding in the cab. They had driven all day across the Delta, on the Louisiana side, making many stops to inquire if choppers were needed, and not having any luck, for it had been dry this spring, all the way up from where the migrants had started in east-central Louisiana where the cotton was planted three or four weeks earlier than it was in Arkansas or north Mississippi. The O'Neal family had started out at Jonesville, and from Jonesville had gone to Jena . . . to Sicily Island . . . to Newellton . . . on into Delhi; and from Delhi to Rayville, to Lake Providence, and finally to Wilmot, Arkansas, then on through Eudora, Parkdale and Lake Village.

Before the cotton was all chopped, Jack expected to see Dermott, Dumas, Gould, Gillett, Wabash, and even West Memphis, following the meandering river northeastward. But as soon as the truck crops began to ripen, some of the families preferred tomato picking around Warren, Hermitage, and Pine Bluff, in July and the first week or so of August, then they'd journey northwestward to pick peaches around Lamar, Clarksville, Coal Hill, Altus, Ozark, and Mountainberg.

In September and early October the first apples are ready for picking around Springdale, Rogers, Pea Ridge, and on into Noel, Missouri, or across to Sleigmann, or back over around Blue Eyes.

Sometimes, the O'Neal family had made more money on the Mississippi side of the Delta, starting out at Natchez, going north toward Vicksburg, stopping off at the little towns and villages in between; and from Vicksburg, to Greenville . . . to Cleveland . . . to Clarksdale, Lula, Olive Branch . . . on in to Memphis.

Mainly, the O'Neals followed the seasons northward, but where they went depended upon the need. Jack remembered the onion fields of New York state, the mucky acres of headed lettuce in the Rio Grande Valley.

"I think they don't want us on account of the goat," Mama allowed, at a time when Jack was driving away from a cotton plantation. And then, "Did you see how that old man looked Nanny Bell over?"

"Yeah, he did," Jack nodded.

But he knew the real reason the cotton farmers he'd seen had turned down his offer to chop. They didn't like the idea of hiring two young'uns and one old woman with no grown man to see to their work.

"When do we stop?" Peggy Jo said again, moving her tired feet to the battered dash so that her dimpled knees were in evidence.

Peggy Jo was as chunky fat as a pig raised on dishwater slop. Her cheeks flamed like ripe Ozark apples, and except for her chubbiness, she was a right pretty girl of twelve.

"A body just has to be patient with baby fat," Mama had said on more than one occasion. "She'll hone down slim and fine, one of these days, like a coachwhip snake shedding his skin."

Neither Jack nor Mama O'Neal had bothered to answer Peggy Jo's question. The old flatbed truck was headed for Delta City. The O'Neals had been coming to Delta City for five summers because it was so far back in the lonesome country that work was always available.

Only one route leads into Delta City, a ragged, washed-out gravel road through miles of desolate swamps, unbroken except for scattered signs advertising Clabber Girl Baking Powder, Burma Shave, Coca-Cola, Grove's Tasteless Chill Tonic, Garrett Snuff, and the local Holiness Church, JESUS SAVES! Narrow wooden bridges span the brackish creeks with the water the color of chewing tobacco. Herds of brahma cattle graze in the swampy places, their fat humps standing up like huge wens on old men's backs. Now and then, you come upon a Negro family walking to —only God knows where, but you remember the sad stares on the stolid faces, seen until they disappear in the brown dust.

"We're coming into town!" Jack said. "Just look how dusty everything is!"

"And lots of dust means no rain, which means no grass," Mama O'Neal said gloomily.

"But there'll be thinning and weeding," Jack said cheerfully. "We'll find work, I betcha!"

Delta City has only one paved street. On it are located the general merchandise stores of red brick, and the courthouse of native rock with the chaw-tobaccos homesteaded on the knife-whittled green benches, filling stations, some still with hand pumps, a drugstore, with a doctor's office up above it, a beauty parlor, a barbershop with a broken pole, a café with two jukeboxes in it, another café with two jukeboxes and one pinball machine; and a public telephone, with no directory, a repair shop, a fishing bait shop, which always seemed to smell of dead minnows; and then you came to the cotton gins and warehouses on the south side, silent now in summer, but with accumulations of ginned waftings on roof and smokestack and in nook and crevice, like dirty cotton candy. In the fall of the year when the diesel engines begin to thump-thump-thump under the tin roofs, waste fiber falls upon housetop, lawn, shrub and tree, like dirty snow.

"We gonna eat before we drive out to Mr. Bob's?" Mama asked.

"It takes cold money to eat in hot cafés," Jack said, assuming the role of his father.

"Well, it's now late, but I reckon a body can get by on beans and bread, if he puts his mind to it," Mama answered.

The truck was then stroking down Main. A chaw-tobacco looked up from his whittling in front of the barbershop to gaze at the old truck, and as Jack braked the creaking vehicle down for the one stop light, Nanny Bell went "Baaaaaaaaa!"

Roosevelt responded with a lusty growl, which caused a barefoot Mexican boy to turn back across the wide street. Before the light changed to green, two tractors bearing trailer loads of Mexicans crossed in front of the truck and headed off down a side street toward Mrs. Maud's Boardinghouse, though Jack knew that most of the wetbacks lived in their battered old fifth-hand cars and trucks, cooked and slept "out." But some big families found it cheaper and safer to stay at Mrs. Maud's. She usually charged five dollars per room per week. Hers was an antebellum monstrosity of many rooms, both upstairs and downstairs, with wisteria vines shading the upper gallery and providing a safe haven for spiders, lizards, dirt daubers, and hummingbirds. At the great steps, one white column had keeled over. It lay in the lush grass like the ghastly bone of some prehistoric monster.

The old women of Delta City told weird stories of the house's past. Mrs. Maud's father hanged himself from the upper gallery in 1923, but before that, after the battle of Tucker's Bend, a couple of Yankee cavalrymen had ridden their horses up the winding stairs, whacking the banisters with their sharp swords, and finding two of Mrs. Maud's great-great-aunts hiding in a clothes closet, made them come out, and despite their pleas, forced them to give up their gold rings, bracelets, and silver plate.

As the truck slam-banged down the wide street, going past the thicket of pecans in back of the ancient manor, Mama O'Neal excitedly pointed it out to Peggy Jo.

"There's that haunted house!"

"Where?" Peggy Jo asked.

"See! Right over there where all of them old cars are parked! That old Fincher woman told me that on dark, still autumn nights you can hear the thunder of them Yankee horses' hoofs on the stairway, the hoarse shouts of the soldiers, and the screams of them two old women when they got caught!"

"Ah, I can't buy that!" Jack scoffed. "Why, you know the wetbacks wouldn't board at a haunted house! And we've seen them there ever since I've been coming to these diggings."

"Watch out, boy! Don't be sassing me!" Mama O'Neal snapped. "I figure the wetbacks just don't know about the house being haunted. Why, as much racket as them young'uns make, I figure the grown folks just can't hear all of that tarryhooting around."

Mama O'Neal was more superstitious than she cared to admit. Jack had seen her walk around ladders, turn over chairs if she heard a screech owl at night, cross herself even though she was not a Catholic, if a black cat crossed in front of the truck, wear buckeye balls for her "rheumatiz," and turn a snake she'd killed on its back during a dry spell to make it rain.

The sun had set. Shadows folded down on the vast cotton fields south of town like a purple accordion. Jack had turned on the weak headlights, which were barely strong enough to allow him to read the sign beside the turnoff.

BOB TURNBOW'S PLANTATION. And there was a yellow arrow pointing.

In another five minutes, they saw the light blurting out of the windows of the modern ranch-style house.

"I just hope Mr. Bob ain't full up with choppers," Mama sighed.

"He'll make room for us, even if he is," Jack said confidently.

As the truck stuttered to a bone-shaking stop in front of the metal gate, a dog came out of the fig bushes at the corner of the house and gave out a sus-picious bark, which set off Roosevelt to barking, Nan-nie Bell to baaaaaaaing.

Then Mr. Bob came to the door, shirtless, his great hairy stomach like an old piece of black cowhide hung on the crib door, and shouted the dog down.

After the hound slunk off behind the house, he called, "Who is it?"

"Mr. Bob, it's us—the O'Neals!" Jack shouted.

"Jack? Is that you, son?" he returned. "Well, where's Wesley?"

There was a little clicking sound in Jack's throat as he got out and crossed to the gate. "Dad passed on, sir. Took down with the ulcers . . . buried him last week, and now we're looking for chopping."

"Wesley passed on? Well, I do say!" And then, "You've come to the right place, son. Here, let me get my shirt and shoes on, and I'll come out and talk business."

"No, we can talk terms in the morning," Jack answered. "You were getting ready to take your shower."

"Well, all right. Go ahead down to the creek to park your truck. There's plenty of room there. Four Mexican families and an old man from Texas. I'm paying five, Jack. Looks like that's all I can afford."

"That's fine," Jack nodded. "Is the hoeing too tough for Peggy Jo?"

"Peggy Jo? Why, I'd forgotten her, nearly!" And he threw up one big, hairy hand, waved at her. "Hidy, Peggy Jo! And you, Mrs. O'Neal!"

"Hidy, Mr. Bob!" Mama and Peggy Jo said at the same time.

"Mrs. O'Neal, I'm sorry to hear about Wesley," Mr. Bob said. "Ain't never been a harder worker than your husband."

Jack knew that Mr. Bob was speaking from his heart, and for a moment he felt a strange closeness to this coarse old man, a widower, who now shaved when he wanted to; a man thick, muscular even yet, with a strongly masculine ruddy face, huge ears, with sprouts of hair growing out of them as tough as cat-fish whiskers.

Finally, Mrs. O'Neal said, "Wesley thought a heap of you, too, Mr. Bob."

"You folks ain't eat yet, have you?" Mr. Bob asked. And before anyone could reply, "I know you ain't! Now, git out and come in! My cook didn't throw out all of the peas to the dogs!"

"Thanks, but we'd better go on down to the creek and pitch the tent," Jack answered. "I want to get in a day's work tomorrow."

Jack knew that the code the plantation owners stuck to did not permit them to take migrants into their homes. For one thing, because of the huge number of fiddlefoots who came during the height of the hoeing and picking season, it would have been impossible to accommodate all. Another reason, social lines were clearly drawn. No self-respecting planter, no matter how well he liked his laborers, could afford to take them into his home.

"Well, if you insist," Mr. Bob continued. "Skeeters ought not to be too bad on account of this dry spell, but you'd better watch out for the wild hogs. They're coming up out of the bottom on account of the sloughs have dried up . . . saw a drove crossing Ben Knight's pasture, just below the place where Tom Woodhall shot that big buck last November."

"I got Roosevelt," Jack answered.

"Who's Roosevelt?" Mr. Bob asked.

"My boxer dog. Remember, he was just a romping pup last fall when we picked for you," Jack said.

"Well, it's a good thing you got him, but remember, ain't no dog alive can match a bunch of *hongry* wild hogs!" Mr. Bob warned.

"You just don't know Roosevelt!" Jack said, confidently. "Well, it's getting late . . . see you in the morning, Mr. Bob."

"Yeah, boy!"

Ten minutes later, Jack was pulling up near the line of cars, trucks and tents. Campfires yet burned in the darkness, and as he braked the old truck to a stop underneath a water oak, he smelled the good gladdening odor of slow-boiled pinto beans, and then he saw the little fire, with the black pot hooked to a tripod above it, the wrinkled, toothless old Mexican woman, with hair as coarse as a mare's mane, hunkered down beside it, stirring now with that slow, deliberate patience of one who knows she's too old to complain.

Other smells now came to Jack's nostrils . . . wild flowers, funky creek-bottom soil, grease, and humanity, as he went around to the tail gate to let it down. Mama and Peggy Jo stayed in the cab of the truck until Jack had led Nanny Bell forth, trembling some as he tethered her to a sapling close by the place where he intended to pitch the tent.

Unloading Roosevelt proved to be a bigger job. The dog seemed half-crazed with joy on feeling Jack's gentle hands on his collar. He leaped and bounded, twisting his rump so, he knocked off a box of Mama O'Neal's empty fruit jars (she canned blackberries in season) which drew an angry warning shout from her as she leaned her head out of the cab.

"Get down, sir!" Jack commanded. But even as Roosevelt's belly flattened against the rough splintery truck bed, he nibbled at Jack's hand, his tongue going like a red-hot windshield wiper. Jack pulled and coaxed him to the tail gate, then made him jump. He hit the ground with a thud, yelped joyfully, then began sniffing among the leaves as Jack tied his chain to a nearby bush.

Next, Jack took out the big battery-powered lantern and hung it on the limb of a tree so that the spotlight glowed warmly on the area that he'd chosen to pitch the tent. As Jack went about the business of cutting new stakes, he thought maybe some of the other migrants would come and help him erect the tent, as this was the general custom, but such was not the case. He was conscious of tarp flaps being drawn back, of being stared at by eyes as dark as chinky-pens, but no one came.

It took a long forty-five minutes for Jack to pitch the tent, even though he'd helped his father each time the family had moved. Then he began to bring out the

O'Neal worldly goods—all of which, with luck, might have brought twenty dollars at a foolish secondhand dealer's.

Mama O'Neal, brushing down her wrinkled skirt, stood looking at the pasteboard boxes, her face wreathed in a violent, mirthless smile. If she loathed anything on the face of this earth, it was moving her meager furniture about; but, with a shrug, she turned to the cab and called, "All right, you, Peggy Jo! Get out of there!"

"Ah, Mamma, I'm sleepy!" Peggy Jo wailed.

"Unpack! Unpack!" Jack yelled, in his excitement not thinking that he might be disturbing his new neighbors.

Immediately he engaged in a sort of dance of unbuckling, untying, and putting chairs, table, field stove, and cots in place. Quickly, he was joined by Mama O'Neal and Peggy Jo, and soon the tent was in order.

Sitting in the chair at one end of the table for a moment in order to catch her breath, Mama O'Neal looked at Peggy Jo, sadly said, "Bring out that piece-of-a-loaf of light bread and the tinned meat. Looks like it'll have to be another *TREET* supper."

"Ah, good Lord, Mama! I can't stand to eat any more of that old canned junk!" Peggy Jo whimpered. But being hungry, did as she was told to do.

Chapter 3

"Jack! Jack!" came Peggy Jo's shrill cry. "Jack! Jack! Get up!"

He was awake instantly, reaching for his jeans, as he slid one leg over the side of the cot, aware that she was standing just outside the entrance, yelling and crying all at the same time, and then she was screaming: "Stop it! Stop it! Take your hands off our dog!"

"What in the world is going on out there?" Mama O'Neal called sleepily.

"Ah, she's probably found some sort of strange worm," he said disgustedly, buckling his belt.

But when he heard the harsh, guttural snarls, followed by the muted choking sounds, he knew it wasn't another green worm this time, and as he ran out, Peggy Jo ran in, her hands over her eyes. They hit head on, right in the entrance, and held on to each other to keep from falling.

"What is it, you little fool!" Jack said, in a frightened tone.

"They're killing Roosevelt . . . all of them mean old

35

men, that's what!" she screamed. "Choking him to death!"

He pushed her aside, ran under the flaps, burst out into the little clearing, and this is what he saw, all in that one horrible moment—three muscular *hombres* holding on to the threshing boxer, throwing him down upon the leaves time after time, as the biggest one of them twisted the collar tighter and tighter, until poor Roosevelt's breath came in anguished gasps; until his eyes bulged out; until Jack saw them ooze blood.

Jack shouted, then he was running, running, and just before he reached the tumbling forms in the leaves, launched his slight body into the air in the classic flying tackle, plunging right into the midst of them, knocking those powerful brown hands loose from the collar which had now become a noose. Then brutal hands pushed him aside, and again the Mexican hombres, speaking rapidly in their native tongue, fell upon the weakened dog, who was sitting on his haunches, his red tongue lolled out, his breath whistling.

Jack saw the big hands strike at the collar again— saw the leather tighten, twist.

"Mama! Oh, Mama! Bring the shotgun!" he yelled.

Vaguely, he was aware that Mama O'Neal and Peggy Jo were standing there at the entrance, their faces tight with frozen horror.

Again Jack moved toward the men and the struggling dog. One turned, held up a fist, warned: 'No, *muchacho!* No, *muchacho!*"

Just then, there was a rustling sound in the bushes, and a bass voice drawled, "Miguel, Ramon, Carlos, git up and leave the dog alone!"

All in one moment, Jack saw the brown hands moving away from Roosevelt; saw Roosevelt weakly stand, then stagger toward the tent; saw the big, old, stoop-shouldered, bow-legged man moving like a massive slow-footed bear toward the clearing; saw the battered knapsack in one gnarled hand, the cocked .45 in the other.

"Boys, I'm ashamed of yawl gittin' aholt of the young'un's dog," the man drawled. "Now, I been fiddlefooting for right close to thirty years and I ain't never seen one of you folks act like this before!"

"Señor Ferguson, thees dog, she snarl at my Susita!" the big Mexican said. "She is wan dangerous animule, Señor Ferguson!"

"It ain't a she, it's a he," Jack said angrily. And then, "But Roosevelt won't bite nobody! He was just meaning to be friendly, that's all! I had him tied good, I thought. Maybe the children set him loose."

"Son, go chain up your dog," the old man drawled. "We ain't wantin to cause me to git riled up just on account of a biscuit-eatin mutt."

"I still say it was their young'uns who turned Roosevelt loose," Jack said. "I know I tied him up good."

It was when Jack was going after his dog that he thought about Nanny Bell. Funny that she hadn't let out one single baaaaa! As he came back to the tent, he looked over at the sapling where he had tethered her. Gone! Goat, rope, everything!

"Mr. Ferguson! Mr. Ferguson!" Jack called. "My goat's gone, too!"

The Mexicans who had now started walking back toward the tents began to laugh and go baaaaaaaaaa! Then they pointed toward the trees where the trucks were parked and Jack saw Nanny Bell looking out at him from the back end of a pickup truck, her head up, still; with fright in her sad, brown eyes.

"Come on, Nanny Bell! Milking time!" he yelled.

The old man, who'd put the .45 back in the knapsack, was staring at the goat, his mouth open. "I Ganny, it's a real live goat, fer a fact!" he boomed.

It was then that Jack noticed the high-heeled Western boots he wore, the way he stood there in the early morning sun, his legs wide apart.

Then Nanny Bell jumped, came running past them, her bell jangling.

"Her bag is as yaller as fool's gold!" Mr. Ferguson drawled. "And as tight as a dead cow's belly."

"I'll give you some of her milk," Jack promised. "Thanks for saving my dog. You looked like a real cowboy, the way you held that big gun."

"The boys got scared, that's all," Mr. Ferguson drawled. "By nature, wetbacks are peaceful folks, just like all folks who labor in the soil. But a man will git some riled if he thinks his young'uns are threatened. Any old pore cow will do the same thing."

"Do yawl get your drinking water out of the creek?" Jack asked.

"Naw. There's a good cold spring over there in that clump of black gum," he said, pointing one maul-sized hand. "Water tastes like it's flowing from the land of milk and honey."

"I got chores to do before I hit the field," Jack said. "Thanks, sir. If I can ever help you out . . ."

"You can help me out by seeing to that dog, boy!" he said. "Just keep him tied up for a spell."

"I will," Jack promised, moving toward the tent.

By seven o'clock, the time the choppers headed for the cotton fields, Jack had a fair knowledge of his surroundings. He had located the spring in the clump of black gum; had got down on his hands and knees, pushing back the leaves, and had drunk like a horse, in huge gulps, then had filled up the thermos jug.

Later, he'd skirted the edge of the bottom for a while, then had walked down to the bank of the creek where the cypress trees sighed in the little wind coming in with the fleecy Gulf clouds and gazed at the swirling water. The creek, no more than fifty feet wide, ran east toward the Mississippi River, through a thick swamp of cypress, gum, and oak.

Coming back through the dense woods, he'd seen several hog signs—fresh earth where they'd rooted up tender shoots, and many tracks in the wallows. Once, as he sprinted past a narrow slough, a flight of ducks got up in front of him and jetted toward the creek, their wings whistling. Then he saw the camp; saw that more cars and trucks had come in while he was away.

Mama O'Neal and Peggy Jo, each dressed in jeans and blouses, were ready to go to the field. He joined them, and soon all three were in the midst of a jostling crowd of choppers, walking across the clearing toward the shimmering green lake of cotton rolling and tossing, the whole two thousand acres of it, in the early morning sun.

Mr. Bob waited for them at the edge of the field, a little black notebook in one hand. Unlike the Delta Pine Plantation eight miles back toward the river, which was owned by a corporation and which, by the use of machinery and chemicals, had eliminated, as far as possible, the human hand, Mr. Bob still held to the old-fashioned ways of his father.

"I like to see my fields clean," he'd say. "Oh, I know chemicals are cheaper, and mechanical cotton pickers, too, but I just can't stand to see all of that grass the chemicals leave—all of that scab cotton hanging from the burrs after them huge behemoths have lumbered through the fields."

There was a sort of foreman named Jet Pinkard the hoe hands had to report to. He was a whiskery chaw-tobacco who kept walking around behind the choppers, looking to see if the less reliable youngsters were cutting out all of the grass and thinning the cotton down some where it was needed.

The sun was pitching the shadows long even yet, as

the choppers dispersed like blackbirds through rows of ankle-high cotton. In the wet places the grass was thicker than the cotton, and cockleburs and Johnston weeds had got off to a good start, but except when they had to kneel to pull out the grass growing among the cotton plants, the work was not too hard, though in less than an hour Peggy Jo was whimpering about the heat popping out on her back. "It feels like I've been wasp-stung all over," she said to Mama O'Neal, who was chopping the row next to hers.

"Come on, girl! Show me sompin'!" Mama O'Neal snapped. "I ain't gonna have you raised up a puny little heifer who thinks she's too good to work."

But when she began to lag behind the other choppers, Jack who'd gone way out ahead, almost even with the most skillful of the Mexican men, moved over to her row and chopped back toward her until he had met her.

"Wish I had a brother to help me like that," came a timid Puckish voice.

Jack turned to see the girl bent over a bunch of cotton, slowly and painfully pulling out the sprigs of grass, blade by blade.

"No way to chop cotton!" Jack called. "Pull all of it out at one time, or let it be! And you can learn to use your hoe more on the opposite side of the row."

"I'm new at this," she replied, looking around at him.

She is a pretty little thing with that finely chiseled face framed by honey-colored hair, he thought. Her

eyes were the color of sandstone, and there was a
laugh in them, as if she found the world about her
funny. The faded jeans she wore had been patched
at one knee, but the seat of them looked almost new,
so you couldn't say she was lazy. Her white blouse,
a bit frayed around the collar, was as clean as a white
kitten's tongue-washed fur.

"Hey, look me over, lend me your ear,
Fresh out of clover, mortgaged up to here . . ."

she sang, and then, abruptly, "Hope you got your
eyes full!"

Jack's face reddened. "Well, I like that! You spoke
to me first!"

"But did I stare at you like you are . . ." and she
hushed.

"Did I stare? . . . Well, I didn't mean to!"

"Oh, I know you think I'm trash like all of the
others," she said. "Well, I'm not! My daddy is a coal
miner, and when he gets his retraining money, we're
going to live in some city."

A tall, pale-faced man, far down on his row, turned
and looked at the girl and said sharply; "Irish, quit
messing around and get to chopping! Do you want the
foreman to dock you?"

"Working as fast as I can, Daddy!" she returned.

Jack began walking down the long row, with most
of the choppers now out in front of him—all except
Peggy Jo, who just had the lags this morning.

"Pssssst! What's your name?" the girl called.

"Jack," he said, stopping, turning.

"Jack? Jack what?"

"Jack O'Neal."

"Then you're Irish, too!" she crooned. And then, "Don't you want to know my name?"

"It's Irish. That's what your daddy called you."

"Yeah, but Irish what?"

"I don't know. Tell me."

"Irish O'Bannion."

"It's pretty."

He began walking again, his feet cuffing up little puffs of brown dust.

"Say, where do you stay?" she asked.

He waved one hand toward the camp. "Over there," he said. "Lot's of folks do."

"We're living in a boardinghouse up town," she returned. "But I wish we didn't."

"Uh, huh."

He was walking again, faster now, aware that Jet Pinkard was coming up behind.

The Mexicans, both the adults and the children, saw the foreman, too, and began chopping faster, and cut out most of their laughing and jabbering.

Jack was then chopping about even with the old Texan, who was two rows down from him. Sweat glistened on his wide forehead below the band of the tremendous cream-colored Western hat.

"You take a bunch of wetbacks, an-ser they're as happy as a tent full of Holy Roller preachers," Mr.

Ferguson said. "By Ganny, they enjoy working, on account of that's all they've ever knowed to do."

"Yes, sir," Jack mumbled.

Mr. Ferguson stared at him. "Why, boy, you ain't paid my words a bit of attention." He began to grin. "Right pretty little Tommy, ain't she?"

"Little Tommy?"

"Yeah. I call all pretty girls Tommy. That was what I called my firstborn, God bless her. Wanted a boy, and she got borned. Pretty as a sack of speckled pups, but I did want a boy! Don't even know where she's living now. I went back by Cut and Shoot, Texas, this past winter, and they'd done moved, her and her husband. I don't know where. Some said to California, but nobody seemed to know."

Jack worked as fast as he could, until his arms felt like they'd break off at the shoulders, and he was soon out in front again.

Then he began furtively eying Irish. Her arms were going like an oil field pump, flashing white above the row of green. She was really trying, but he knew she'd be fagged out before quitting time. Chopping cotton is hard work, even when he was used to it, he remembered. But during those first few days of the season, it nearly killed him. His arms and shoulders and neck always hurt, and his back, if there was much stooping.

"Why, a body feels just like she'd been throwed from a horse them first three or four days!" was the way Mama O'Neal put it.

As the sun lifted higher, Jack's shadow almost disappeared. Soon, a sawmill whistle blew far down the flats, announcing the noon hour. "Twelve o'clock! Dinnertime!" Mr. Ferguson bawled.

"Dinnertime for some folks, but just twelve o'clock for me!" a colored man shouted.

Work stopped, paper bags were opened, cups were filled with ice water at the big barrel in the back end of Mr. Bob's pickup. Some of the Mexican mothers went to the edge of the field and held their babies awhile. Some of the older children, once they'd eaten their meat sandwiches, played cowboys and Indians, and when they tired of that game, Tarzan and the apes, running back and forth through the heat-drooped cotton, laughing and shouting. Some of the Mexican men gathered in little football huddles and talked of cockfights. Sometimes, dice were rolled in a clean-raked spot; sometimes, a pack of greasy cards was produced from a sweaty pocket, and a poker game began.

At one o'clock, when work resumed, and the salty meat sandwiches in the children's stomachs cried out for water, there was an endless line of brown feet moving back and forth to the water barrel, kicking up choking clouds of fine dust which sifted into eyes, ears, and lungs. Sand streakers, striped and serpent-eyed, made their runs through the cotton rows, making the women shriek with fear that they'd run up their legs. Once, a coachwhip snake, a muddy brown in color, came winding its way across one end of the field. The children threw down their hoes and chased it through the cotton. Jack was the first to catch up with it. He struck out with one hand, seized the rusty-looking tail and whirled the snake above his head, with the children shouting, "Pop its head off! Pop its head off!"

"Watch it!" Jack yelled, as he flicked the snake outward, like it was a horse whip, jerking it sharply, which popped off the narrow head. He saw the head flying like a frozen, stiffened bird across the cotton field . . . saw it falling into the green sea of cotton.

Jack pitched the quivering, writhing, undulating headless length down upon the hot earth.

"Turn it on its back, and it'll rain before morning!" Mama O'Neal called.

"Better still, go hang hit on a barb-wire fence, and you'll have good luck till Saddidy," an old Negro man advised.

"Naw, I'm not superstitious," Jack grinned, going back toward the place he'd left his hoe.

There was no shade, not even a persimmon tree in the field; only vast, stretching rows of cotton, which seemed to run on to the end of the earth. Heat waves danced with fiendish glee out in front of Jack. Then, he got to listening to the sound of his hoe . . . scraf-ah, scraf-ah, scraf-ah! . . . an endless numbing rhythm. Arm-breaking, neck-kinking!

Some workers talked with the choppers in the next row. Some retreated into sullen silence. Jack furtively eyed Irish O'Bannion at times and did some thinking. His duty was quite clear. His father had asked him to take care of the family. He had made the promise to a dying man. That was the reason why he kept helping Peggy Jo with her row, where she could keep in hailing distance of the other choppers. "An-ser, that's a right smart good ideer," Mr. Ferguson drawled, noting the way Jack was helping her. "What a fellow does in this life—what keeps him gitting up in the morning and answering the seven o'clock whistle—is hope! You take hope away from me, and I'd go back to Cut and Shoot, Texas, and git on the old age."

Jack knew that the old man meant the Old Age Pension. Once, during a bad season of no work, Jack's father had talked about finding a house, settling down, and getting on the welfare until he could find a steady job, but he never did do it.

"Son, a man is born to hustle," he had said to Jack. And then, "I reckon I've got the same restless blood in me that Great-grandfather had when he decided to leave Ireland. Our people are just not the settling-down kind, and I can tell you—all of them folks you see traveling around in them big, fancy aluminum house trailers are fiddlefoots at heart."

What worried Jack most was the thought of not being able to find steady work. Two hundred and forty-seven dollars was a lot of money to try to rake and scrape up, over and above eating, gas and oil for the truck, especially when the migrants had to travel hundreds of miles to find work, and go for weeks without any work at all. With luck, steady work, Jack knew he could pay back Colonel House, so he bowed his neck to the hot sun, his arms going like pistons, until the sweat ran down his legs and dripped into the hot earth, and it was then he recalled a saying of his father: "I'm in the soil of seventeen states, my sweat is, and if it hadn't been so cold in Maine, the time I tried to pick apples there, the total would be eighteen."

As the evening sun went down across the purple-hued flats, and quitting time approached, some of the choppers began to sing jukebox songs, some hymns . . .

"Cheer up my brother, live in the sunshine;
You'll understand it, all by and by."

The Mexicans sometimes sang plaintive songs in their native tongue, in the peculiar, jerky rhythm, but usually they began to gather in sniggering groups as four o'clock approached. Once, Jack's father had told Jack about the time, only a few years ago, when the wetbacks had to work a ten-hour day for three dollars and even less. But the government had passed a law limiting the working time to an eight-hour day, though even yet most of the planters didn't pay the minimum scale.

"All right! Quitting time . . . quitting time!" Jet Pinkard called.

Hoes stopped cutting grass. A clot of choppers made a rush to the pickup, because the planters paid off each day, a custom that went back to the time when fiddlefoots didn't stay in one field but a day or two.

Jack stood near the pickup with Mama O'Neal and Peggy Jo. He looked across the field. Irish was following her parents to the truck. Her feet dragged, and the blouse was stiff with brown dirt now, and not starch. But her eyes were smiling.

"You earned your money today," Jack grinned.

"I'll earn it tomorrow, too!" she snapped. "And it won't be more than a week until I'll be chopping just as much cotton as you can, Mr. Show-off!"

"Irish! Don't speak like that!" her mother said, turning to Mama O'Neal with an apologetic smile on her thin lips. "We came from the city, you know. Irish has never worked in the field before."

"Yes, I reckon a body could tell she hadn't," Mama said icily.

Jack looked at Irish's mother. She was thin, angular, with a rather pretty face framed by light brown hair. The dress she wore looked like it was a size too small, and she had made the mistake of wearing hose to the field today, and nice shoes.

"All right! Next!" Jet Pinkard called, holding the time book in one hand.

"I wonder if he'll dock the children?" Mrs. O'Bannion whispered, as she stepped up some in the line.

"Naw. Mr. Bob is a fair man," Mama O'Neal snorted. And then, "They tell me the old rascal is fixing to marry again!"

"If he does, we ort to shivaree the old cuss!" Mr. Ferguson boomed. He was standing three places down in the line, his big Western hat in one hand, his foul-smelling pipe in the other.

49

"Why is that, Mr. Ferguson?" Mama O'Neal asked.

"Well, I figure it this way, folks," Mr. Ferguson boomed. "The first time a man marries, he don't know what he's gitting in to, but the second time—he ort to pay for it!"

There was a little shower of laughter from the choppers, then Jet Pinkard was saying, "Next!" And the line began to move again.

Late that afternoon, right after he'd come in from blackberry picking, Jack decided that he wouldn't tie up Roosevelt at once, but would sit out with him, watch him, and make sure the frisky dog didn't bother the Mexican children, who were scattered throughout the woods above the spring, like several coveys of quail.

For a time, Roosevelt didn't try to sneak off, but lay sprawled out underneath the truck bed, licking the scratched places on his feet and legs. Jack was right proud of himself. He had picked two gallons of berries after he'd gotten off from work, which he would sell for seventy-five cents each tomorrow when he went in to town for ice. Not much money, true, but every little bit would count, as he was determined to pay off his father's debt.

Mr. Ferguson came out a little later to talk to Jack. He was in a languid mood, with his stomach full of well-done steak, French fries, apple pie, and coffee, for he'd eaten supper in town. He had a newspaper in one hand, his pipe in the other.

"Man, I feel good this evening," he said. "Like I had the world in a paper sack and standing on top of old Smoky!"

"Money in your pocket makes you feel good," Jack allowed. "But I reckon even that won't make Peggy Jo happy. None of the kids in this camp will play with her."

"Oh, they will in time," Mr. Ferguson answered. "That dog of yo'rn is a fearful-looking rascal. He stands as high as a yearling calf, an-ser he's got teeth as long as a grizzly bear's. But young'uns will take up with anything nearly, give 'em time."

Jack eyed the tent. Peggy Jo sulked there. She had tried to make friends with three Mexican girls about her own age that afternoon, so Mama O'Neal had told him. "Why, she even brought out her Barbie doll, the one your pa bought her in Florida on her birthday, and that broken wristwatch that Mis' Clara give her while we was down in south Mississippi, and them uppity gals still wouldn't play with her."

Jack knew the Mexican girls didn't have anything to be uppity about, with hardly more than the ragged clothes on their backs, pallets spread down on leaves or warm earth, and a diet that consisted mostly of pinto beans. No doubt it was the fear of Roosevelt that was holding them back.

Except for the shrill cries of the children roaming through the woods beyond the spring, peace had settled upon the land. The sun had gone down behind the wall of timber rising up out of the dense creek bottom. Not a leaf moved on the water oak trees, nor bird, nor insect. From a distant slough there came an incessant glee-ank glee-ank-gluk-gluk-gluk of frogs.

Jack lay back on the earth and through an opening in the trees watched the sky alter—from pale blue to orange, and then to purple and gold. Pictures ran through his mind, like it is at the theater, only the ones he saw were live, real: His father coming home from town, bearing the sack of peppermint, peanut brittle, juicy-fruit gum . . . proudly . . . so proudly! Like the hunter coming home with the fat buck . . . so many towns, all different, and yet alike, too, with their red-brick courthouses and chaw-tobaccos sitting on the green benches whittling and staring out at the street! And home—what had it been? A tent pitched near a stream, with mosquitoes whining outside the tent flaps. Sometimes, baked beans for breakfast, dinner, and supper. But in season, catfish fried to golden honey bubbles, and squirrel mulligan—and baked coon, with sweet potatoes and gravy.

How long would he continue to listen to the sounds of him? . . . His voice calling with increased urgency, "Jack, time to git up, boy! Jack, son! Git up!" The way his rubber boots squeaked in the dew-wet grass in the early morning when he searched for Nanny Bell.

Ah, but for a little time . . . a little time! Soon, he would listen for his father's voice no more; he would hear the sounds of him, never more!

Suddenly a scream broke the peaceful calm, and as Jack sprang to his feet, Roosevelt took off like a brown rocket, right through the thicket, guttural growls coming from his great throat.

"What in the Sam Hill was that?" Mr. Ferguson boomed.

He had tossed his newspaper aside, had clambered to his feet, the heels of his boots biting into the soft earth, looking toward the thicket. Then Jack was off, sprinting through the brush, for now he heard the unmistakable sounds . . . WUF WUF WUF! Wild hogs! Jack ran lightly through the thick woods, his slim body flashing forward in the dim light. Ahead of him, some one hundred yards, the hog sounds were louder, and now he heard Roosevelt's angry shrieks and growls. Jack ran faster, shouting, yelling—heard the screams of the children, the increased furor of the hogs and dog. He was lashed by tree limbs, scratched by briers, and held by vines; yet he ran on, hearing the din of noise, and now louder than anything else, the squalls of the children, and behind him unintelligible shouts . . . and then a *mujer* calling, "Susita! Susita!"

And then he plunged out into the clearing in the midst of the affray, tripping over a limb, going down face first into the loamy earth. But in that brief moment, this is what he saw: five children milling around underneath a beech tree, shrieking with terror; children already up the tree—children climbing the tree; and between the children and the hogs, vague, leathery shapes, their heads held low, a little foam issuing out of their mouths, over near the edge of the clearing—Roosevelt! Roosevelt, with his big paws widespread, so that his shoulders and chest were almost touching the leaves, his head up, his strong, white teeth bared, his ears flattened, baying angrily.

Jack jumped to his feet, ran to the children at the tree, and helped them climb upon the first limb, one by one; then he was looking around for a club, tree limb, anything that would do for a weapon. The wild hogs, three sows, and one old boar, with a number of pigs hid out somewhere in the brush, looked thin, hungry. They had no intention of going without their supper.

Jack was desperately feeling around in the leaves in search of a pine knot, shouting at Roosevelt all at the same time: "Come here, boy! Good boy! Come here, dog!"

But Roosevelt followed his instinct. In Germany his breed of dog had been used in a sport called bearbaiting because of their fierce, determined courage.

Roosevelt forgot himself, caught up the way he was, in the ecstasy of the hunt.

The dog did not cry out, but drove upon the mean old boar, shoulder shocking against shoulder, so hard that he forced the boar back against the grunting sows, his gleaming teeth striking into the scarred hide of neck and shoulder.

With a hoarse snort, the boar bounded back, struck Roosevelt so hard in the chest that the dog went down, the wicked, foam-flecked tusks missing the dog's throat only by a fraction of an inch. They rolled over and over in the leaves, teeth and tusks slashing, cutting. Once, Roosevelt cried out, and Jack felt his heart race. He'd seen dog-hog fights before—had seen a bluetick hound get its belly ripped open, from chest to abdomen, as completely as if a butcher's knife had been used!

"Roosevelt!" he screamed. "Come here! Come here!"

Roosevelt gained his feet first, and then he was darting in, slashing the boar down the shoulder and leaping clear. Jack heard the teeth of his dog snap together like the jaws of a steel trap, as he backed, feinted, rushed, retreated, and all that time the old sows, their heads down, and chewing their teeth until foam oozed, were going wuf-wuf-wuf.

In a flash, Jack knew it was a fight to the death— that he had to help his dog, somehow. He'd picked up one limb, but it had broken in his hands, and now he was desperately searching for another one. Vaguely, he was aware of the shouts back in the wood toward the camp; of the ghostly calm in the clearing. The children didn't let out the faintest whisper, nothing moved, not a leaf, twig—nothing but the dog and the boar, circling, feinting, rushing in.

In vain the big boar tried to hem Roosevelt in, knock him off his feet, but Roosevelt eluded him, his fangs striking into shoulder and rump and belly. Then, suddenly, Jack saw the boar change his tactics . . . instead of rushing in, saw him slash out with those deadly tusks . . . saw Roosevelt's shoulder streaming blood, heard him panting hard, and then he found a sturdy tree limb, with last year's leaves still intact and rattling like gourd seed, as he rushed into the melee . . . saw the mean old sows suddenly start up, plunge into the fight, knocking the dog to the ground.

Jack swung the limb harder than he ever had a baseball bat, hard against the tough snouts of the wild hogs—against back and belly, the blows making a hollow, drumming sound. And then, he had separated the old sows from the boar; beaten them back into the bushes, as they roared wuf-wuf-wuf. During that time, Roosevelt and the boar had rushed together with their teeth and tusks snapping and slashing. Once, Roosevelt yelped; once, the old boar squealed; and then Jack was aware of loud shouts, of running and threshing about in the woods.

"Back up, boy!" came Mr. Ferguson's booming voice. "Back up a little ways, son!"

All in that brief moment, before he started walking backward, Jack saw it all: the old Texan, the .45 in one hand, aiming it, trying to get a bead on the head of an old sow; and Roosevelt, his strong jaws locked, his teeth deep in the boar's throat. Even as he heard the choking gurgles of the dying boar, the .45 blasted out flame, smoke, and sound, and the old sows lit out—grunting and squealing, picking up their "hid out" pigs, as they made their run to the creek, and to safety.

Then Jack saw the circle of men around the struggling dog and dying boar; heard their excited chatter.

There was no hope for the boar. Mercy was a quality that Roosevelt reserved for his loved ones. Even when Jack grabbed his dog's hind legs and tried to pull him off the old boar, the jaws held.

"Leave him be, son!" the old Texan said. "He won the right."

Jack looked around to see the old man, his legs wide apart, calmly blowing the smoke out of the barrel of the pistol, and now, looking back at the boar, he saw that the leg kicks had grown weaker. He stood there, watched the lean, pointed hoofs calm down to a tremble, then cease to move at all.

It was only then that Roosevelt released his hold, got up, staggered back, blood still streaming from his shoulder and his left ear, panting hard.

"Good boy!" Jack crooned. "Good boy!"

"Your ma's gonna have to sew up that ear," the old Texan allowed. "If you don't, maggots will git in it."

"Come on, boy!" Jack said, patting the bloody head, then bending to examine the shoulder.

But Roosevelt kept twisting and turning, his tongue lolled out. The best Jack could find, the cuts were superficial.

The Mexican hombres were then helping their children down from the tree, talking excitedly, and as Jack led his dog back toward the camp, he met several women. Mama O'Neal was in their midst.

"Just as well get out your needle and thread, Mama," Jack said. "Got to sew up Roosevelt's ear some."

"Ugh!" Peggy Jo cried, and high-tailed it toward the tent.

"Come back here, you little fool!" Mama cried. "A little blood ain't gonna hurt a body!"

But Peggy Jo kept on running. Jack was glad she did, for that time he'd stuck the tenpenny nail in his foot in the old barn where he and Peggy Jo had gone to kill rats, she'd taken one look at the crimson streaming out of the round hole and had promptly fainted.

Once they'd gotten back to the camp, Jack brought out the lantern and Mama O'Neal came with her threaded needle. Jack held his dog, talking low and saying flattering words into his ear, and even though Roosevelt winced with pain, his stump of tail never did quit wagging.

When she'd finished at last, Mama O'Neal grudgingly admitted that Roosevelt was a pretty good dog. "I reckon we couldn't do without him," she said.

Jack had already gone to bed, though he was still so excited he couldn't get off to sleep, when he heard the car pull up outside the tent, then heard the unclear voices.

Roosevelt gave a warning growl. Jack heard a voice say, "Good *perro*! Good dog!"

In a moment Jack was up, easing toward the entrance. He pulled the tent flaps aside, peeped, saw the three men standing near the tree where Roosevelt was tied.

"What do you want?" Jack asked.

It was the big Mexican with the powerful wrists, the one who had choked the boxer. He was holding out a sack.

"Have no fear, muchacho," he grinned. "Thees ees Miguel. We have been to town. We have brought sometheeng for your perro."

Jack got the lantern, turned it on, and came out. He took the sack. It felt limp, and smelled of fresh bloody meat. He opened it up—saw three thick slices of sirloin steak.

"But this is too costly!" Jack said. "Naw, don't take it from your Susita!"

"Eet ees for the perro, muchacho!" Miguel smiled. "If not for heem, maybe I wouldn't have no little muchacha!"

Jack looked at him doubtfully. He was almost afraid to refuse the offer.

"Thanks," he said. "Roosevelt sure does love fresh meat, but he ain't used to this kind of a feast!"

"Feed him, muchacho!" Miguel said.

"No, you do that, and make friends with him," Jack returned. "Ain't nothing like food that will make a dog forgive."

Chapter 4

Jack sold the blackberries for a dollar a gallon early the next morning when he drove into town for fifty pounds of ice. It happened that the man who owned the icehouse and filling station loved blackberry jam, and when Jack inquired of him about potential buyers, he stepped around to the truck and had a look at them, bought them on the spot.

"I'll buy a lot more, if you pick the good ones like you did these," he promised.

"I'll fetch you some more tomorrow," Jack answered.

As he drove along the narrow road, Jack felt a lot better than he had since his father had passed. If the chopping held out, in time he could pay off Colonel House, but beyond that, his future plans were dim. One time the visiting teacher of a high school in Louisiana had come to talk to him. She made education sound mighty good, but he hadn't promised her anything.

"I can force you to come to school," she'd warned. "But I understand how hard it is for ah—migrants to make a living. But it seems to me that you must choose between education and fiddlefooting. A few more years, and you'll be too old to finish up high school. All you'll have left is the life you now know, and if the machine keeps on replacing the hand in the fields—well, all you'll be able to do is get on the welfare."

"I got to stick with my family," Jack had replied. "I can't settle down, if they don't."

The lady had talked to Jack's father, had tried to persuade him to settle down for the sake of his two children, but he wouldn't promise anything. "I tried settling down once, and I nearly starved," Mr. O'Neal had returned. And then, "I'd rather roam the back country than get on the welfare."

Dad is gone now. If I just had enough money to pay Colonel House, I could really settle down, Jack thought. A little farm was what he wanted, near a creek or river, just close enough that he could catch a school bus. But the family had to eat! There was no settling down now.

But his prospects seemed brighter. After Roosevelt had killed the boar, the Mexicans had become almost too friendly, with little brown girls and boys running in and out of the tent even before breakfast, until Mama O'Neal had to shoo them out. "Like a bunch of brown leghorn biddies, just running ever which of a way!" she had grumbled, once they had gone back to their tents.

But she had been pleased that Peggy Jo now had someone to play with during the hours when they were in the tent. "It just makes a body feel warm inside to know her baby is happy," was the way she'd put it.

Jack did not see the O'Bannions at the cotton field when he went to work, but there were a number of new choppers, brown and hard, who brought word of burned-out crops where they'd been chopping, on the Mississippi side.

But around nine o'clock the O'Bannion family came to the field. Irish deliberately walked past Jack. This morning she had on new jeans, another white blouse, and a new straw hat.

"We had to move out of that boardinghouse," she said to Jack. "Bedbugs nearly carried us off last night."

"Where did you move to?" Jack asked.

"I don't know. It's a little shack-of-a-place out on the edge of town," she answered. "But even that beats fighting off bedbugs—and roaches! My goodness! They hung on those bedsprings in clusters, like grapes!"

As she walked on toward the end of the rows, Mr. Ferguson muttered, "Ain't she a pretty little thing, though! An-ser, when I was a boy yo' age, I'd of rasseled a grizzly bear and give up the presidency of the United States just to hold her little hand!"

"Huh, city folks!" Jack snorted.

"Listen, boy! If I was in yo' shoes, I'd be nice to her, no matter if she come from Mars!" he boomed.

"I ain't got nothing to be nice to her with," Jack said. "Nowdays, it takes cold money to be nice to a girl."

"Why, foot! Take her fishing! Take her berry picking, son!" And then, "A pretty little gal ain't as interested in money as you might think! Why, she don't know a consarned thing about woods and creeks. Take her fishing!"

"I'll think about it," Jack promised.

"Take her the first time it rains," Mr. Ferguson advised.

The trouble was, the dry weather held on—and on. Out of the cloudless skies, the Deep South sun poured down unmercifully, and then when night came, it wasn't much cooler.

"It's the humidity," Mr. Ferguson explained. "Now, you take where I lived in Texas . . . it got up over a hundred lots of times, but it was dry heat! That old river"—and he pointed toward the Mississippi River bottom—"is what does it. Just too much moisture in the air!"

The first thing Jack gave Irish was some wild grapes, and the next thing he fetched her was some locust shells. You could stick them on your nose and face. "She got right tickled when you hung that one on her nose, didn't she, son?" Mr. Ferguson asked.

"They ain't nothing that feels as scratchy as a locust shell!" Jack grinned.

Two days later, after the thunderstorm blew in from the southwest, turning the field into a billowing lake of water and mud, Jack took Irish blackberry picking. Of course Peggy Jo and the grinning brown-faced Susita had to tag along, too, and Roosevelt, who went sniffing through the wet bushes, though his nose was not keen to the fresh scents of swamp rabbit, coon, and possum, for he was not a trailing dog.

For three hours that afternoon, carrying their empty lard buckets (empty at first) in their hands, the little group went laughing and holloing through the deep woods, stopping only when they came to the patches of blackberry vines, then pushing in, keeping an eye out for the deadly swamp rattlers, which had the reputation of loving the deep shade of the briery vines, and then picking rapidly, their hands flashing in the dappled light.

They told silly jokes, and asked silly questions, like What did the cat say when he saw the two-hundred-pound mouse coming down the alley? and tried to scare each other by making strange noises, got eaten up by red bugs, hung by ticks, scratched by briers, lashed by limbs, struck by bushes, lassoed by vines, and had a wonderful time, in a way only teeners and children can.

"We'll try it again sometime," Jack promised as he walked with Irish up the meandering road which led to the camp.

"The next time it rains!" she nodded.

"Good! I hope it rains all the week!" Jack grinned.

As it turned out, it didn't rain again before the chopping was finished up on Mr. Bob's plantation. Already, in the late evenings, the migrants were talking of the chopping prospects in northeastern Arkansas.

And then, Mr. Bob, jubilant over the prospects of a good cotton crop, up and married!

"A mere young'un at that!" Mr. Ferguson had said, half in jest, once he'd seen the bride, a big-eyed, fine-figured Delta girl, who'd given every indication that she would be an old maid until Mr. Bob proposed to her.

Of course, no sane girl could turn down Mr. Bob. He was the richest planter in the Delta, even though nobody would have guessed it, once they'd heard him try to pray down at the Holiness Church. It was a fact that the old cotton farmer, as rich as he was, couldn't read.

Jack had once heard a courthouse chaw-tobacco bait Mr. Bob with, "Brother Bob, could you explain that scripture in the Bible where it says, Blessed be he who sitteth upon the hot stove, for he shall surely rise again?"

Mr. Bob had mopped the sweat off his red neck, cleared up his throat as if he would explain the scripture, then said, "Ah, I don't believe there's nothing like that in the Bible . . . blame your time, Harlow Welch!"

Mr. Ferguson, so Jack believed, was the first man to mention shivareeing Mr. Bob. For one thing, the field hands talked about it all day, and that evening, when they went into town for ice, they spread the news everywhere.

"Mr. Ferguson, just who all goes to a shivaree?" Peggy Jo asked, only minutes before those who'd planned to go got their stuff ready at the camp.

"By Ganny, everybody goes who wants to!" Mr. Ferguson snorted. "That's one shebang where you just can't have too many on hand."

"I'm going, then!" Peggy Jo said, looking at Jack as she spoke.

"Sure! Come along!" Mr. Ferguson invited. "This is going to be the daddy of all shivarees that's ever been held before! Old cuss knowed better!"

It seemed to Jack that nearly everyone who lived in Delta City had gathered in the pine thicket behind the tractor shed, and as the crowd waited, Jack learned a great deal more about the old farmer.

This one would make his fourth marriage. The reason he'd run through with the other three women was that he'd made them slave themselves to death taking care of the old farmhouse, an ugly thing, with two huge rooms set on either side of a wide hall, with an L-shaped dining room and kitchen tied onto the back. The folks who'd gathered there in the thicket declared the only reason Mr. Bob had built the new house was to get someone to marry him.

The fact that Mr. Bob had several thousand dollars on time deposit up at the First National Bank didn't seem to increase his popularity, either, and this puzzled Jack. From what he was hearing, Mr. Bob seemed to be two people—the fair-minded man the migrants knew, and the hypocrite, skinflint, and woman killer that the Delta folks knew!

The shivaree, Jack decided, was not going to be done in sport and good humor, as much as it was in revenge, spite, hidden resentment.

At first no lights were showing in Mr. Bob's new brick-veneered house, as the crowd built. Mr. Ferguson expressed his doubts that Mr. Bob was at home.

"Oh, yeah, he's in there!" a stranger said. "It's just that he's starting Lou off right—training her to keep that consarned electric bill down!"

It seemed to Jack that the crowd had doubled in size in a fifteen-minute period. The way the cars, pickups, and horses were parked along the highway, it looked like a big funeral. Only a few of the Mexicans had come to the shivaree. They kept well back in the bushes, and although they didn't fully understand what was fixing to take place, as Mr. Ferguson issued new instructions the word went out like waves on a pond . . . . "All right! Get your implements ready!" Mr. Ferguson boomed, and all down the line, to the place where the Mexicans were hiding, men, women, children, passed the word along.

It is more like an Indian raid, the way we're creeping up on the house, Jack thought. Peggy Jo kept wanting to stand up and walk, but the old Texan would have none of that. "Git that gal down on her all-fours or send her home!" he said, gruffly.

"Oh, me! I've run into a bull nettle!" Peggy Jo moaned.

"Just scratch hit and shut up!" Mr. Ferguson snapped.

The air around the new house was pungent with the smell of crepe myrtle, oleanders and red roses, flowers Mr. Bob's other wives had put out over the years, for he'd been very careful to preserve the flowers and trees while the new house was being built, and had fired three different sets of carpenters before he'd found a crew who'd cooperate.

"Let 'er rip!" the old Texan boomed.

All of a sudden, the dark was ripped by whoops and screams and pistol blasts. Then the hunters came on with their automatic shotguns and drowned Mr. Ferguson's .45 out. People were up, running, banging on dishpans, plows, washpots, tubs, bull drums; and one old codger from the other side of Delta City was blowing a Civil War bugle handed down to him by his grand-daddy, and it all added up to such a terrible commotion that the Mexicans broke and ran toward their fifth-hand Buicks, babbling in their native tongue.

Under cover of the noise, Peggy Jo began to cry, and in his haste to be the first to reach the bridal bower, Mr. Ferguson tripped over a cultivator rusting in the weeds outside the yard, and when he fell, it was into the arms of a local giantess, who stood an even six-two, barefooted.

69

"Watch hit, Grandpa, or you'll *swaller* your false teeth!" she said in a voice as deep as a V. O. Stamps bass singer.

She lifted him like a skillet and set him down heavily on a spiked-toothed harrow that had been turned bottom side up. He let out a roar of pain, came up rubbing himself with both hands, and for a long moment, Jack was afraid he'd shoot the big woman.

But the commotion in the weeds had stirred up a hornets' nest. The giantess suddenly let out a hoarse yell and took off running through the persimmon bushes slapping at her sitter at the same time. For a moment everyone turned and watched her flight toward the barn.

"Hit sounds like a tornado has hit in a red oak thicket!" Mr. Ferguson said. "And if that noise don't bring out Mr. Bob, nothing will!"

Just then, hornets began to buzz in the weeds. Mr. Ferguson yelled a warning. "Everybody for himself!" And he took off, running toward the horse trough. Then everyone ran.

Peggy Jo, her teeth chattering as if she had a bad chill, kept up with Jack until the giantess, who was well out in front of the crowd, ran into the clothesline and nearly burst her goozle. The reason Mr. Bob had the clothesline propped *that* high was to keep the goat from chewing the legs of his long-handled underwear, and the reason he had his longhandles out in the summertime was because of the wool suit he'd got married in. He always wore the longhandles summer or winter, when he wore the wool suit, to keep it from scratching his skin, but, of course, Jack didn't learn about this until the wealthy cotton farmer told about it in the field the next day.

"Oh, I've killed myself!" the giantess hoarsely moaned.

He saw her turning and twisting and writhing in the grass, her hands tearing at her throat, and that was when he ran off and left Peggy Jo, rushing to the big woman's aid. Jack had always gone out for football at the schools he'd attended, but of course he never did make the starting lineup because the coaches were always afraid he'd move off in the middle of the season. But he had learned a few pointers about first aid, and he knelt beside the threshing giantess and pushed against her chest until she had caught her breath.

She finally sat up and Jack asked, "Feeling all right now?"

"Yep," she nodded. "But, Lord what a lick! I ain't been hurt that bad since the night I fell in the dug well over at Caledonia!"

"All right, everybody! Let's get going!" the old Texan bawled.

The crowd had regrouped near the pine pole Mr. Bob had erected for his TV antenna. In spite of all of the noise, not a light had been turned on in the house, though Mr. Ferguson explained to Peggy Jo that this was the local custom. A party getting shivareed wasn't supposed to give an inch! Let them tear down

71

the door, knock out all of the windows if they would! "Of course you don't ever destroy property!" Mr. Ferguson said loudly, for the benefit of some of the more radical elements who'd joined the party.

Peggy Jo clung to Jack like a grass burr. "Let's go home!" she begged. "I don't like these old shivarees!"

"Go home, my hind foot!" the old Texan roared. "Why, the fun is just fixing to begin!"

"I come here to eat!" the giantess said hoarsely. She seemed to have fully recovered. And if anything, she looked even taller than she had before, or so Jack thought. Could the jolt she had gotten have stretched her neck? He smiled when he thought about it.

"I say, when do we eat?" the giantess said, again.

It was a long-standing custom for the couple getting shivareed to give treat, provided enough noise was made to get them up out of bed, so Jack was told by Mr. Ferguson in the field the next day, at a time when they had been chuckling over the night's to-do.

"One more time!" Mr. Ferguson yelled. "Give it to them, and make them know we mean business!"

What had gone on before was mere child's play. Everyone had pressed right up to the house, though being careful not to stamp down the flowers growing along the walls. Tubs boomed, bull drums bellowed like a herd of angry bulls, shotguns blasted out sound and smoke, women gave out cat shrieks which were enough to make the hot blood of a hummingbird run cold.

"All right! Hold everything, folks!" Mr. Ferguson said.

He walked to the steps, reared back and shouted, "All right, Mr. Bob. We know you're playing possum! Come out and show that pretty little bride, and give treat!"

"Open the door . . . open the door!" others began to chant.

The next minute Mr. Bob turned on the porch light and came to the door, his flour-sack nightgown (one of a batch his first wife, who was a good seamstress, had made for him) hanging over his overalls.

"Just a minute, folks," he said, sheepishly. "Give the little woman time to get the goodies on the table."

"So you was expecting us!" the old Texan roared.

"Yep. I heard all about it uptown late this evening. There's cigars for the men, ice cream and Coke for the women and young'uns, and plenty of hospitality for everybody."

"Well, what are you waiting on?" Mr. Ferguson said, impatiently.

"I'm so hongry I could eat a steer on the hoof," the giantess boomed.

"Well, come in!" Mr. Bob said nervously.

All bedlam broke loose inside the house as the crowd poured in. Mr. Bob's fourth wife, a silent young woman with pale, Holiness lips, but rather pretty, stood near one end of a huge homemade table, nervously seeing to the needs of men, women and children. Matches scratched against the bottoms of worn

overalls and jeans as the men lit up the cigars—even
the men who didn't usually smoke; caps popped off
Coke bottles; children stood impatiently in a line
leading to the ice cream freezer, beating the bowls
they held with their spoons, and the ones who'd gotten served first had already gone outside and were
amusing themselves by scaring Mr. Bob's white leghorn hens out of the pear tree in the backyard, then
running them down as they fled cackling and cluck-
ing toward the barn.

Mr. Bob high-tailed it to the back door and shouted
at the young'uns until they went home.

Inside the house, the men stood in little football
huddles, and spoke of crops, fishing, narrow skirmish-
es they'd had with the local game warden, and the
probable time of the coming of Jesus Christ. The
women stuffed themselves with ice cream, swigged
Coke, and harried the young bride with all kinds of
advice concerning the canning of Blue Lake snap
beans; told her three ways to deep-freeze purple hull
peas, how to shop for groceries down at the big chain
store on Thursday's (double-stamp day), and argued
with her about the Scriptures, explaining the difference between Solomon's wives and his cucumber
vines. Then, the giantess, a Coke in one hand and a
bowl of ice cream in the other, made the mistake of
trying to sit down in Mr. Bob's TV chair, a ladder-
backed, cowhide-bottomed one, with the rungs nearly worn in two where he'd propped his bunion-
knobbed feet.

The old Texan described the way the giantess had fallen, in the field the next day—"It was like a sawed-down tree," he said. "An-ser, she hit the floor all at the same time, with ice cream falling everywhere like manna from heaven!"

The way the giantess got up sputtering and threatening to do bodily harm to the first person who laughed was what really broke up the shivaree. Men, women, and children had to laugh or burst, so they bade quick farewells to the bride, thanked Mr. Bob for the treats, and ran outside, clabbering the still night air with hooting laughter. Even men who hadn't laughed since the time a Republican ran for governor of the state folded over in the yard, with the seats of their overalls pointed straight at the moon. Ladies, who were supposed to be too mannerly to laugh at the misfortunes of others, reared back and howled like dogs hearing a train whistle.

As the crowd went back across the pasture Jack, now caught up in the full spirit of the shivaree, slipped up on Mr. Bob's old Jersey milk cow, who'd been standing under a chinaberry tree beyond the tractor shed, jumped astraddle of her, and she lit out across the pasture, bucking and twisting sideways, churning her own butter. But Jack stayed on her until she suddenly came to a jolting stop, stood on her front legs and kicked at the sky.

The first time Jack came down, he lit on the cow's neck. The next time he landed, it was in the grass, so hard on his sitter that he bounced like a basketball.

Then Peggy Jo was standing over him, asking over and over, "Are you all right, brother? . . . Are you all right?"

"Just winded," he groaned, picking himself up slowly, and walking with his sister toward the old truck.

Chapter 5

Choppers were leaving the Delta City area in caravans of fifth-hand cars, pickup trucks, and flatbeds, following the northeastward route, where the cotton was planted later by several weeks than it was in the south Delta region.

Mr. Ferguson had about persuaded Mrs. O'Neal to follow his old Chevvy to central Arkansas where the tomatoes were just beginning to ripen, he said. He argued that the farther up the Delta you went, the smaller the cotton allotments, and a chopper would spend most of his time moving from one field to the next.

"Why, you folks can make more money for less work," he said, late one evening when the last of the wetbacks were leaving the camp. "And we can live in houses most of the time. Getting skeeter-et just ain't good for growing youngsters, and it don't help my bones any to sleep in my car or on the ground."

"Wonder where the O'Bannions are going next?" Jack asked.

"Shoving off in the morning . . . going up the Delta," Mr. Ferguson said. "I tried to tell O'Bannion he is making a mistake, but it didn't do any good. He's not one of us. A man can't work twenty years under the ground, then come out and expect to know how to earn money on top of it."

As it turned out, the O'Bannion family was in the field the next morning, ready to help wind up the last of the chopping. Jack looked around and saw Irish coming up behind him, chopping fast, trying to catch up, on the row next to Mr. Ferguson's. Her face was flushed, for the sun was so hot it would make freckles on tadpoles, with the sky cloudless, deep blue; but she was clean, neat, very pretty. "The Tommy looks like she just stepped out of a bandbox," Mr. Ferguson sniggered. "I bet she bathed twicet before she come to the field this morning."

"Water boy! Water boy!" Mrs. O'Neal called.

She was standing so that she leaned on her hoe, her stiff finger sticking out like the stop on an organ, and as she waited for the water boy to come from the truck, she pulled off her straw hat and fanned her sweating face.

"It is a hot one, ain't it?" Mr. Ferguson said to her. And then, before she could reply, "Mama told me there was going to be days like this, but I didn't believe her. Ah, how sweet it was to be young, then! I was eating my white bread and didn't know it."

"Water boy! Water boy!" The cry went up in the field, as the choppers kept the colored youth hopping.

"I got the fantods, Mama," Peggy Jo said, with a whimper.

"It's hot, young'un, but don't whine!" Mama O'Neal said. "I just don't think I can stand to listen to a whining young'un this morning."

Jack deliberately slowed down where Irish could catch up with him. Her arms flashed like pistons, but she didn't sweat much, except over her upper lip, a tiny line, like beads, and then she was speaking.

"I've been trying to talk Daddy into going where you people are going," she whispered.

"I thought you was telling me that your old man is going back to Tennessee," Jack returned.

"He is when he gets his retraining money. Boy, will I be glad! Oh, how I do miss my TV programs!"

"The Mexicans put the aerials up on their trucks," Jack answered. "At least, some do."

"And eat pinto beans to do it!" she returned.

"You ain't too good to eat pinto beans!" Jack said, angrily.

"No, I'm not, Jack, but I don't want to have to eat them all my life. Do you?"

"A man's life is set—that's what my daddy always said," he answered. "You can't do anything to stop the way you're going, no more than you can look up there at that big ole sun and command it to quit shining so hot."

"I can't buy that!" she flashed. "I think that man is the master of his own fate, Jack. You don't have to follow the roads! You can do something else."

He thought of the promissory note held by Colonel House. "In my case, I can't," he answered. "I'm hooked just as certain as a catfish on a big set hook!"

"Just as soon as we save up enough money, Daddy is going to pay for his own retraining," Irish said. "But he keeps saying the government will furnish it. I don't know, myself, but I do want to get back in school this fall. I'll be in the tenth grade, Jack. What grade would you be in, if you went?"

"That's my business!" he said, tightly.

"You did get to high school?"

"Yes."

"Well, you're still young enough to finish, no matter what grade you got to."

If I could have stayed in school regular, I would be graduating next year, he thought. But he didn't continue the conversation with Irish, for he remembered fifty different schools, thousands of different faces, some of them unfriendly, some looking down on him. Trash. That was what they thought the migrants were! Lazy, shiftless, dirty, dirty-minded, ignorant, stupid, living out of tin cans and filthy cafés. In those schools he'd attended briefly, he'd always been an outsider. To even think of school gave him an uneasy feeling, like it was when you thought about going to the dentist to have that sweet tooth yanked.

The students at those strange schools just didn't know. They didn't understand that the migrants were like other people, mainly; living, eating, having fun, thinking about the future, just like other people.

Jack listened to Irish beg her parents all morning. "I don't want to chop any more cotton!" she kept stubbornly saying. "I want to pick tomatoes, peaches, apples! It'll be so much cooler in the Ozarks, too!"

"But that would be going away from Tennessee and home!" Mrs. O'Bannion snapped. "I want to get back there by fall. I've got my flowers to see to, and if that start of St. Augustine grass dies from the lack of water, I'll want to reseed the lawn."

"You know we are not going back!" Irish snapped back. "You know how Daddy has started back to drinking again—and if he goes along where that Webb family goes, he'll stay soaked all the time, just like old man Webb!"

"Don't argue with your mother, Irish!" Mr. O'Bannion said. "We're heading for Tennessee. You might as well shut up!"

It was then that Irish began to cry, sobbing silently for a time, ashamed to let the other choppers hear her, and then crouching down in the brown dust, beating the hot earth with her tiny fists, crying, "I don't want to go where the Webbs go! I don't want to go!"

It was a scene Jack would always remember, the way her face was wretched with sorrow, stretching her lips until her little white teeth were bared; the way the hot tears dripped into the dust like little drops of rain, in that flat hot stretch of green running off into a hard blue sky. Near a bunch of cotton a small red ant struggled with a bug twenty times its size, and down two rows, a baby kildee bird lay dying, its wings stiffening, its wretched little feet quivering feebly, and bleeding a little from its frail breast where someone's hoe had cut into it, accidentally.

Tragedy stalks in the lives of all creatures, in all small corners of the earth.

The O'Bannions left that afternoon. Their old Ford was loaded down with bedclothing, pots, pans, skillets, suitcases full of clothing, and all kinds of little items that Irish had accumulated during their travels, and as the car passed by the cotton field, where Jack and his family, Mr. Ferguson, and two families of Mexicans were hoeing the last few rows, Irish leaned out the window and waved one hand at Jack. "Goodbye," she said, sadly, lurching with the roll of the car as the wheels hit a hole, and then she put one hand to her lips and blew him a kiss.

"It'll be a cold wind in August when we see them again," Mr. Ferguson said. He was standing there, his heels apart, staring at the old car kick up the brown dust.

"It's best for them, all the way around," Jack muttered. "They just ain't the fiddlefooting kind."

Chapter 6

In Hermitage, Arkansas, Mr. Ferguson found an abandoned café for rent on the outskirts of the little town. The closest house was at least a mile away, which suited Jack fine, because he wouldn't have to be watching Roosevelt so closely, and he could take the rope off Nanny Bell's horns where she could roam at will through ditch and slough and across bushy field, cropping grass where it was sweetest.

The café, one of those quick and get-rich schemes of someone who'd found that there just wasn't sufficient traffic to afford enough customers to keep it open, was new, large, and fairly comfortable.

Each morning they went out to the tomato patches below the little town as the sun peeped over the piney hills and green slopes and joined others, then picked the Louisiana Pinks, Arkansas Reds—and them half-green, for they would be shipped out by the co-op to far away cities. The odor of the tomatoes got into the pickers' clothing and hair, and the peculiar pink-ish dust turned their hands to the color of the yellow stripe down the center of a paved road, not all at once, but gradually, over several days of handling them. The pay was by the hamper. The faster they picked, the more money they made.

Jack made better than five dollars most days, while Mama O'Neal did well if she made more than four dollars. Usually, Peggy Jo picked three dollars' worth, except on her sulky, puny days, and then she sometimes made less than two.

Jack had already mailed in a money order to Colonel House for ten dollars, with a short note promising more soon if the work held out, and there was enough money left for the family to eat some meat two or three times each week. Occasionally, Jack slipped around and bought Roosevelt a bag of choice bones for thirty-nine cents, then hid the sack out in the pine thicket behind the abandoned café.

Each day, Jack walked past the packing sheds and looked at the new faces of the migrants who'd just come in, hoping to see that one face he so longed to feast on again—Irish's. But hers was never among them. There were all kinds of faces, to be sure—brown Mexican faces, blond native Arkansan faces, black Negro faces—but never that one face that he sometimes saw so vividly in his dreams.

It was during those dark days of loneliness that Jack began to walk the one street of the little town, mostly at dusk dark, for no adventure book, no Western movie, no crowd, no sunrise or sunset would drive off the smothering despair; for he thought he knew he'd never see Irish again.

The walks reassured him, for a little time, and he came to know the scrawny tomcats in the alleys, the town drunk, the slow-walking lovers, and the town marshal who eyed him suspiciously at first, until he learned that Jack meant no harm.

But always, he had to return to the café, to bed, and to the nightmares about things that might happen to his family, and to Irish. One day passed another, and it didn't get better.

But a day did come that was different . . . the day Deputy Sheriff Whitey Nolan drove up at one end of the tomato field in the dusty official car, got out, and strode across the long rows until he came up to the first of the pickers, who eyed him suspiciously.

Jack heard the deputy sheriff clear his throat a time or two, then heard his question: "How many of you people out here are from out of state?"

Some of the pickers shouted the names of the states they had been across. Some ignored the officer and kept right on picking.

"I'm from Texas," Mr. Ferguson boomed. "But what difference does it make?"

"Ah, some state mess," the deputy snorted. And then he told the pickers about it. Because of the trouble a migrant had given the school authorities in a nearby county, one day a deputy sheriff came to the tomato field and announced to all of the laborers who called themselves migrants that they'd have to come up to the courthouse to get interviewed, though none of the fiddlefoots knew why they were being interviewed until days later.

The fiddlefoot who'd settled down on a farm simply refused to let his children be vaccinated for any of the childhood diseases. He belonged to the Holiness faith, and among other things, he thought that Christ had already come again; that it was a sin to contaminate the human bloodstream with vaccine taken from an aging mare.

Anyway, the two psychiatrists came down from the state capital, promptly borrowed five dollars from the sheriff for Coke money—they'd both forgotten their billfolds—and started the interviewing. As soon as Jack had taken the tests they let him go back to the field, but Mr. Ferguson had to spend the whole afternoon there in the funky-smelling jury room behind the table, while one of the psychiatrists questioned him.

The old Texan told about it the next day in the field.

"Why, he didn't no more look like what a psychiatrist ort to than a cow looks like a mule!" Mr. Ferguson said. "He was off, you know, not an idiot or anything, but he warn't right, I can tell you! His eyes was as big as two-dollar-and-a-half watches, and just as dead-looking as a fish's! An-ser, I reckon he stared at me nigh on to a half hour, not saying a word, just looking, so I finally said, 'You finished looking, you can pick up your eyeballs! I sure wouldn't want to step on them.' He said 'awp,' like he'd been asleep or sompin', then set right in to staring at me agin, them eyes as big as a gator's, and just as greenish-looking. So I stared right back at him. At last, he reared back in his chair, said:

" 'Are you a Holiness?'

" 'Nope, but I know a preacher out to the tomato shed who is,' I said. 'He told me the reason he had to take to the road was that his mule never did come up last spring. I asked him if he ever did look for the mule, and he told me, no; if the good Lord wants me to plant a crop this year, he'll see that old Beck comes in. Well, here it is in July, and old Beck still ain't come.'

"An-ser, this psychiatrist looked at me a long, long time, like I might have been a detour sign on a lonesome road. Then he said:

" 'Where you from?'

" 'Texas,' I said.

" 'Don't people from Texas lie a lot?' he asked.

" 'Yeah, they do, but no more than people from other states,' I said.

" 'What do the people out there think about vaccinations?' he asked.

" 'I ain't heard them say nothing either way!'

" 'Do you believe in it?' he asked.

" 'Yeah, I believe in it—for other people,' I said. 'But you can't pay any attention to the way I feel about anything. I believe in the United States of America, though that ain't none too popular in this age of the sheep and the lion lying down together.' "

The old Texan squinted his eyes at the sun, to gauge the time of day, and continued: "Then he started asking all kinds of things I had done as a child, where all I had been, and a bunch of downright foolish stuff which I couldn't remember nohow, and suddenly he leaned forward, shoved a bunch of ink spots in my face and said, 'Look at this a long time and tell me what you see.'

"An-ser, all hit was, was ink spots, but when I told him that, he got right mad at me, and he said, 'Keep looking until you see sompin', if it takes all evening!'

"Well, I finally figured out what he wanted me to do. I reckon I just hated to disappoint him, the way he was wanting me to find sompin' in them spots besides ink, so I lied to him. 'I see an iron lung,' I said.

" 'What else?' he asked.

" 'And, ah—hit reached down into a cave.'

" 'Okay. What else?'

" 'And there's a womern in hit—a scared womern with little wens on her neck and back!'

" 'Yeah. What else?'

" 'And she's whipping a bunch of little babies . . . all kinds of little babies with a black pattle!'

" 'Yeah? What else?'

" 'That's all I see.'

" 'Very well,' he smiled.

"An-ser, he was right pleased with hisself. I reckon he'd already seen what I claimed I had, for he shore did smile, and all. I thought hit was all about over, an-ser, the fool leaned across the table on his elbows and said: 'What is hot?'

" 'How's that?' I asked.

"I didn't think I'd heard him right, but he come right back at me with:

" 'What is hot?'

" 'Hot is like the sun is this evening,' I said.

" 'What about fire?' he snapped.

" 'Well, of course fire is hot, too!' I said.

" 'What is cold?' he then asked.

" 'Like ice is,' I said.

" 'What about water?' he asked.

" 'Cold water is cold; but hot water is hot,' I said.

"I reckon he thought about that answer for a good five minutes. I saw him fiddling around with some papers on his desk, then he got right personal with me.

" 'Mr. Ferguson, you didn't never marry because you hated your mother, didn't you?'

" 'How's that?' I asked.

"Hit was a question that seemed like hit was loaded on both ends.

" 'You never did marry because you hated your mother, is that right?'

" 'Well, I ain't never thought about hit in that way,' I said.

" 'You mean, you didn't want to think about it, period!' he snapped.

" 'Well, Mama always told folks I was her pet.'

" 'Yeah? Did you ever stay away from home at night until you was thirty-five or forty?'

" 'Oh, yes. I ran away from home when I was eleven . . . been on the road ever since.'

"There was a look on his face like I might have led him up a blind alley, but I'll say one thing—he tried!

" 'Mr. Ferguson, how many of your relatives had to go to state institutions?' he asked.

" 'You mean, be put away?' I asked.

" 'Yeah. You can call it that.'

" 'None that I know of.'

" 'Careful, now! You mean, not a single one of your relatives acted kind of queer or anything?'

" 'Well, now, I reckon I had two uncles what you might call queer-acting. I remember Uncle Chuck. He come back from World War One with an overcoat, which he wore all the summer with it so blamed hot you could feel your eyebrows crawling. I asked him why he wore it even in the summer, and he told me as long as he kept that overcoat on, he wouldn't have no bad luck, die or anything, and hit must—'

" 'That's enough on that!' he cut in.

" 'Wait a minute!' I said. 'I ain't told you about Uncle Ham! Uncle Ham liked to git down on his all-fours and tree squirrels like he'd seen hound-dogs do!"

" 'Aren't you putting me on?' he said, squinting his eyes at me.

" 'Putting you on what?' I asked.

" 'Putting me on . . . putting me on! Trying to make a fool out of me!'

" 'Your ma and pa did that to you,' I said.

90

"He laughed some when I said what I did, then he began staring at me right queerly again. All of a sudden, he leaned forward, said, 'You didn't marry because you didn't like girls, right?'

"'I ain't said I didn't marry! The fact is I did marry, and come close to doing hit twicet—to a widder womern in Clovis, New Mexico!'

"Well, I reckon that floored him. 'All right! All right!' he said, and did he begin to fill out them forms!

"But I wasn't through, not a-tall! 'Feller, I says, I've enjoyed jawing with you a right smart, but all of this to-do about one pore migrant who don't want his young'uns to git vaccinated is a bunch of tomfoolishness.'

"'All right! All right!' he said.

"'There's always been crackpots, and there always will be,' I says. 'But, I've been all over the whole country in my time, and I'm here to say most of the folks in the United States of America are sane, level-headed citizens, no matter what they do for a living; no matter the color of their skin, or how much money they got in the bank.'

"'Yes, yes!' he muttered.

"'Once, I heard the frogs croaking in a Louisiana bayou, and says to myself, this is the place I like where the fishing is good, the womern pretty, and the coffee strong, and then I slept out under the stars on a highway leading through the Dakota badlands, and heard a mountain lion scream out in a lost canyon. This is the place where I belong, I said.'

" 'Yes, yes! Okay, okay.'

" 'But I didn't settle down at none of them places, because I love it all . . . ever dad-blasted inch of it, from Maine to Florida; from Florida to California— and clean up the coast, all the way to Washington!'

" 'Okay, okay.'

"He was cramming papers into his briefcase, not paying me a lick of attention.

" 'Glad to have helped you out, because I'm a typical American,' I said. 'But the next time you want to talk, don't pick the tomato season. I lost right at three dollars this evening.'

" 'Okay, okay,' he said, an-ser, he got up and took off, like he didn't know I was in the room. Well, I picked up my old hat and come back to the field."

From central Arkansas, toward the end of July after the tomatoes gave out, Jack, Mama O'Neal and Peggy Jo followed Mr. Ferguson into the Ozark Mountains, stopping right in the heart of the peach country. The hills, slopes, and valleys were dotted with peach trees loaded with great coppery Elbertas, Chinese clings, Indian reds. Their odor pressed upon the countryside, as the trucks continually streamed from field to packing sheds.

The sun was hot, but usually it was two or three degrees cooler in the Ozark Mountains than it was in other parts of the state. At night, Jack and his family sometimes needed blankets, and the work didn't seem to take so much out of them. Peggy Jo didn't have the fantods so often, and Mama O'Neal slept better at night.

While in the back-country regions, Jack came to know a Mexican girl of eighteen who studied all the time she was off from work, getting ready to take the test required before she could become an American citizen.

She studied history and civics mostly. At night, when the campfires had burned down to ashes, she liked to sit back and discuss the country.

"You people take so much for granted here," she'd say. "But you have so much of everything, I guess you have to do that to get to the important things."

The girl's name was Rita Alvarez. She spoke English very well, indeed, because she had attended American high schools in Texas and Florida. Her parents had planned to go back to the town of Las Quatro Milpas in Mexico as soon as they could save up a little money, but Rita was determined not to return to her native land.

"I have a boyfriend in Miami," she said. "He is waiting for me to get back there. We're going to marry and attend the University of Miami together."

So he watched her night after night sit under the one light bulb near the campfire and pore over the books she had on history and citizenship, then when the fire had died down, and the laughter of children was heard no more, listened to her soft, sibilant words:

"We hold these truths to be self-evident: that all men are created equal; that they are endowed by their Creator with certain unalienable Rights; that among these are Life, Liberty, and the pursuit of Happiness . . ."

Down the highway came the sad thrumming of a juke box in the Ozark Café, and as night folded down on the sleeping camp, he thought about her words, mouthed them softly; tasted them with the buds of his tongue, and then swallowed them deep in his mind, his self. This dusky girl with the Bible-black hair, burning eyes, hauntingly beautiful face had a goal, a purpose. She would go before the court and be tested by the judge, and he had no doubt in his mind that she would win full citizenship.

And the thing is, this is something you already have, he told himself. *But even then he felt that happiness was something more than following Roosevelt through a brier thicket after work was done and the sun was low; that seeing to the needs of Mama and Peggy Jo was not enough. He had a destiny other than following the fiddlefoots in their endless rounds of the nation. If only he could save a little money! Back to school, and if they bought a little house, plowed a small garden, and if Mama and Peggy Jo put out crimson rambler rosebushes in the yard, then the students in the school wouldn't consider him an outsider any more!*

Next morning Jack was roused out of peaceful slumber by the barking of Roosevelt. There was shouting, snarls of the dog, and then someone crying hoarsely, "Come call this dog off! Come call this dog off!"

"Jack, go see!" Mama O'Neal yelled. "Roosevelt is gonna bite whoever it is, for a fact!"

Jack was up, out of the bed, running to the entrance of the tent. He saw Roosevelt, his hackles up, and standing over on the other side of the flatbed truck, the strangest-looking man he'd ever seen before.

"Come back here, dog!" Jack shouted, peeping out at Roosevelt, the way his chest was touching the ground, the way his lips curled back from his big white teeth.

During all the time Roosevelt was retreating, snarling deep in his throat, Jack was looking the man over. He had on a purple suit, the exact shade of a funeral-home awning, a giant of a man, more than six-four, with shoulders broad and angular, and seeming to leap out of the strained fabric of the purple jacket, and with a face that was unlike any Jack had seen before, because of the way the high cheekbones stuck out like two puff adders, and in the way the ashen cheeks seemed to be sunk inward like an emaciated cadaver's. A beaked nose leaped out from under the craggy forehead, above which laired a buzzard's nest of black, coarse hair.

"Hidy, boy!" he boomed. And then, striding toward the tent, "My name is Ralph Waldo Emerson Sikes, but everybody calls me Traveling Man."

His hands, which were as big as his monicker, held a large black Bible. His eyes, whenever he opened them wide, glowed like Roman candles.

As he came up to the entrance of the tent, he began thumping the Bible with one finger. "Say hidy to the Book, boy!" he commanded.

Jack hesitated for an instant, then timidly said, "Hidy."

It made him feel foolish. He wanted to run back inside the tent, but just then Mama O'Neal came out, brushing the wrinkles out of her old field-soiled skirt.

"Good morning, dear Sister!" Traveling Man boomed. "Could you spare me a minute of your time?"

Jack backed into the tent. He'd seen revival preachers before, but none like this one!

"Yes, sir," Mama answered.

"I'm a preacher, as you can see, Sister," he boomed. "Just pitched my tent up at Ringo City, and I thought I'd invite all of the pickers out to meeting. It starts at seven o'clock, rain or shine! Tell everybody, ah . . ."

"Ain't you Ralph Sikes, the faith-healing man?" Mama O'Neal asked, a note of awe coming into her voice.

"Yes, I heal and I save, with the help of the Book!" And he began to thump the Bible again. "Tell everybody to come out to my tent tonight, if they like good preaching and singing! Lord, I got a woman soloist who can make the Devil himself shed his horns like a buck! Her words sound like they're coming right out of the windows of heaven!"

"I guess maybe we can, if we get in from the peach orchard soon enough," Mama answered.

"Do come, dear Sister in Christ! Ah, me! Many will want to come later, when it's too late to come!" he boomed in a sorrowful funeral voice.

"Won't you stay for breakfast?" Mama O'Neal asked.

"And He was a stranger, and they took Him in!" he roared. And then, "No, no! But thanks, dear Sister . . . ah, what is your name?"

Mama O'Neal told him, and Jack heard the fateful words: "Even if you can't come yourself, Sister, you ought to see to that boy getting out there to the tent! All young'uns are as full of sin as a Christmas turkey is dressing! And if you know any sick one—any lame, halt, blind person at all—do send him, Sister! I don't heal, but, ah, yes . . . God does! Sweet Jesus, through me, and of me!"

Then he was striding past the tent, going down to the big camp where the Mexicans were just then eating breakfast, now singing in a powerful, organ-like voice:

"What a fellowship, what a joy divine,
Leaning on the everlasting arms . . ."

"Who in the world was that?" Peggy Jo called, sleepily.

"The Healer!" Mama answered, coming back into the tent. "Now you get up from there where we can get out to the orchard! We got to get an early start if we quit in time to bathe and dress up for meeting."

"I don't want to go!" Peggy Jo answered, as she slid one chubby leg to the floor.

"I don't see why not!" Mama O'Neal snapped. "Church will do you a heap of good. I don't know much about the Scriptures, but I do know a body feels a heap better after a body goes and hears good preaching and singing."

Mama O'Neal had a weakness for revivals, as did most of the migrants, except the Mexicans who were mostly of the Catholic faith. Jack remembered tent meetings in several different cities that they'd attended. She had been impressed by a twelve-year-old boy preacher named Brother Elvis, who not only preached to the teeming multitudes in South Hot Springs, Arkansas, but for the benefit of the teeners, took up an electric guitar and sang religious songs to a rock-'n'-roll beat. Near Oklahoma City, the family had attended a famous faith healer's meeting, and she'd fainted in the arms of Jack's father when she'd seen goiters as big as cantaloupes disappear under the touch of that famous man's hands.

At water breaks, Mama O'Neal talked of the meeting, but Mr. Ferguson spurned the idea of going to hear a "healer."

"He just might cure you of that growth you got on

your neck," Mama said, slyly. "For all I know, it's a skin cancer."

"Ain't nothing to it!" Mr. Ferguson snapped. "If I git to wanting that little bitty wen removed, I'll go to a doctor."

"Well, it won't hurt you to hear some good preaching," she said. "I really think that Traveling Man has got the call! I've heard tell of him for years, but this is the first time I've ever had the chance to go hear him in person."

"I knowed a faith healer who got jailed in south Florida for killing a young'un," Mr. Ferguson said, doggedly. "Kid had had TB of the bone for years, and his parents brung him to the meeting, and the preacher did make him throw his crutches away, and all that, but from the shock of hit, a week later he was dead!"

"Well, all I'm going to do is hear the preaching anyhow," she said.

"Mama, I have been feeling kind of puny lately," Peggy Jo spoke up.

"Yeah, especially when it comes time to go to the field," Jack said angrily. "If he can heal you of laziness, you orta go!"

"Oh, I hate you, Jack O'Neal! Oh, I wish I was big enough to whip you!" Peggy Jo cried.

"Both of you young'uns shut up!" Mama O'Neal snapped. "A body wouldn't even think you are brothers and sisters, the way you fuss at each other! Both of you are going to that meeting! It'll do you good!"

Chapter 7

On the small stage inside the big tent, Traveling Man stood under the golden wash of the spotlight listening to the sad mewing of the organ, and watching Sister Bessie Sweet, his soloist, who was dressed in the purest white, as she worked with the "saved" and thus, the "healed."

Jack, sitting with Mama O'Neal, Peggy Jo, and Mr. Ferguson in the folding chairs down front, was watching the crowd which had come in to Ringo City from miles around. There had long been a murmuring in the audience, mostly women talking in tongues.

Soon after that a cool August wind began to sneak in at the open sides of the tent, stirring up the dust, until there was such a siege of hacking and coughing that the organ was drowned out.

As the choir hummed and the voice of the organ softened, despite the distraction of the women talking in tongues, Traveling Man reared back, cocked his eyes at the very top of the tent, and said:

"Praise His sweet Name!"

"Praise His sweet Name!" the audience mimicked. Maybe Traveling Man smiled a little, but not for long. His was a dead-serious service. He stood raw-boned, solemn-faced. Then he opened up the great coffin-black Bible and held it up and waved it like it might have been a flaming sword.

"Speak to this Book!" he thundered. "Say hidy to it!"

"Hidy, Book!" came a roar of voices.

"Bless you! Bless you!" Traveling Man cried.

Bedlam might have been a quiet birthday party as compared to what followed. Some two hundred women screamed in unison, as if they had rehearsed together. Chairs banged against chairs; feet shuffled; hands reached out fervently, like Traveling Man might be the Great Lord Of Hosts.

Jack had been to many meetings somewhat like this one before, and he'd come prepared not to be *moved*. But he was moved, even as Mama O'Neal was moved—as Peggy Jo and Mr. Ferguson were moved. Peggy Jo had folded her chubby hands against her chest. Mama O'Neal was moaning fitfully, while Mr. Ferguson squirmed in his chair like he was sitting on live coals.

"Praise His sweet Name!" Traveling Man boomed. "He loves you tonight!—Ah, He loves you! And I love you!"

This set the crowd on fire. They murmured Traveling Man's name. They sang it! They lipped it into their hot mouths and trilled it with their ruby tongues! Praised him! Some men and women suddenly leaped up out of their chairs and began to chant, saying words that meant nothing to those who did not belong to the Holiness faith.

All at once, Traveling Man did an about-face. "Sinners!" he yelled, pointing a finger as big as a corncob straight at his audience. "I call you Sinners! Sinners!—Because you're praising me, when you ought to be praising our Sweet Saviour!"

There was a guilty period of silence, complete silence. Jack looked around, saw the way the old Texan was leaning forward in his chair, his mouth open, as he gawked and foofed.

Traveling Man now stood tall and slim, his strong legs planted apart. He suddenly put the Bible down on the table, seized the mike like it might have been a chicken's neck which he was fixing to wring, his eyes burning like Roman candles.

And then, in a singsong chant:

"I have come among you tonight, ah . . .
To heal your weak bodies, and to save, ah . . .
Your immortal souls, ah . . ."

He raised one big hand.

"The power is, ah . . . right here, ah . . .
Coming directly from God! . . .
Praise His Sweet Name, ah . . .
And I ain't no man to get swelled up, ah . . .
Just because I got the power!"

Right after that, Traveling Man went into a terrible recounting of how he had discovered that he had the power.

He spoke of how cancer of the lungs had got him down; told all about how much he'd bled, how the doctors in all of the hospitals he'd been in had given up on him, and how close he'd come to the graveyard —Jack could almost hear the squeak of the rusty gate, see the tombstones—but all of that was nothing compared to what else he told!

When he was just turned twenty-one, he'd had an awful hemorrhage. His father had found him dying in the charity hospital, or he'd thought he was dying, and when the doctor came, the doctor announced he was dead. His body had been carried to the morgue, laid out. And then he told a hair-raising account of how he'd awakened, looked around and seen all of the dead folks, and how he'd begun to pray, and that was when he'd felt the *power*. He'd gotten up and walked out of that deadhouse! And he'd had the power ever since!

But he wasn't through, not by a long shot! He couldn't top that, but he tried. He told all about the people he'd saved, the scrapes he'd gotten into, and how he'd gotten out of them, and the wickedness. Ah, yes. Sin! Sin!

Suddenly, a bent, trembling old man with stuck-out eyes was shouting, "I stole the five pounds of butter and four dozen eggs out'n the school lunchroom! But

I swore under oath I didn't! Oh, yes, yes, Jesus! I done
hit, Jesus! I done hit!"

"Sinner, bow down yo' head!" Traveling Man thundered, pointing a trembling finger at the man's
wretched face.

Jack saw him fall into the dust, his head between
his knees.

"All of you out there!" Traveling Man thundered.
"Get down! Kneel! You've got to pray for this sinner
so God will forgive him before He gives me the power
to heal. Get down!"

Many sprawled into the aisles, hands clasped, pray-
ing fervently. Jack looked around to see his mother
join them. Jack felt the sweat break out on him; felt
the cold chills run up and down his back.

"It's a-coming!" Traveling Man roared. "God is for-
giving this poor sinner, and I feel the power! It's in
my shoulder—now I feel it driving into my arm and
hand!"

"Jack, he sure does know the Book, don't he!" Peggy Jo whispered.

"Right smart!" Jack nodded.

Nearby, a woman stood up, her eyes rolled upward,
exposing the whites. "I done it!" she breathed. "I told
my husband that it was his children, by his other
wife, who killed the Plymouth Rock rooster! And all
the time, it was mine and his'n that done it!"

"Pray for her! Pray for her!" Traveling Man roared.

And, Lord, how they did pray! Men, old men,
women, little young'uns!

And then, when the revival fire had burned out, suddenly, like a burnt-over sedge patch, Traveling Man began to wave his maul-sized hands. "It's coursing through me! I feel it in my shoulder!" he boomed. "You prayed for your Brothers and Sisters, because you, *you* are their keepers! And God has given me the power! And you've come here tonight to see God's power at work, through me, and you're going to see it, too!"

"Oh, glory, glory!" Many shouted.

"Glory to God! Halley-lou-yah!" came other cries.

Traveling Man's assistant, a lovely lady with a sad, wan face, dressed in a flowing nylon gown of the purest white, directed the bringing out of those who'd come there for the healing ceremony, men, women, children. Those with crippled feet, arms, backs, hands; those with great, open sores, some of them oozing corruption; women with goiters the size of pomegranates in their wizened necks; those with cancer-eaten faces, standing weak and half blind, so sick that they were unaware of their own ugliness; men, women, and children wearing dark glasses, having to be led to the front of the platform.

Except for the sad tone of the organ, then the clear, lively voice of Sister Bessie Sweet singing "Let Your Light Shine Out," Traveling Man's ceremony then took on the aspects of a side show, though there was one thing brought home to Jack, and to all who had come to the meeting: Traveling Man was sincere! He believed in himself! And he showed that for the better part of an hour.

"Bring out the first one," Traveling Man said, quietly.

The lady in white led a youth forth from the crowd's crush. He was sweating. He was pale, gaunt, with a corpse's face, and with a great, swollen head, the ghastly evidence of some unusual disease. He had on faded jeans and a ragged dirt-black T-shirt.

Traveling Man then took charge of the boy, lifting him with those powerful arms upon the platform, and then helping him to sit down in a folding chair in front of the moiling crowd. The great head kept leaning forward, as if the stalk of neck that supported it was broken. Traveling Man cupped the trembling chin with one hand, held the head up, then he looked into the youth's eyes.

"What's your name, son?" he said, gently.

The lad tried to speak, but his words, if they were words, came out unclear.

Traveling Man shoved his face at the still crowd. "See this poor boy!" he said, blinking the tears back. "All of them doctors have give up on him! They say the water will keep collecting on his brain until it bursts, but I'm come here, dear ones, sent by my Master! I ain't give up, for the Lord never gives up!"

"Jesus, have mercy!" the crowd moaned.

Traveling Man stripped off his purple jacket, cast it aside. Then he laid one hand on the bulged-out head, moved it, and all in the same moment, his face became set in a look so strange, so terrifying, that Peggy Jo began to cry.

"Shut up, girl!" Mama O'Neal hissed. "Now shut that up!"

It seemed to Jack that it was Traveling Man's eyes that held the boy and the crowd, even more than his hands did . . . eyes that shone, glowed, like a swamp rabbit's at night suddenly struck by a beam of light.

Traveling Man's hand moved, trembled, as he reared back, looked straight up and cried out in a loud voice at the top of the tent, and through the tent, beyond the tent, calling on God:

"Heal him, Lord!" And then, more loudly. "Do it! Right now, Lord!" And now a command . . . "Do it! Do it! Do it!"

"Praise the Lord!" the crowd sang out.

Again the hand moved on the wan forehead, and now sweat broke out on Traveling Man's forehead.

"He's healing him! Oh, He's healing him!" And then, gasping, "I feel His power! I feel it in my right shoulder—now it's flowing into my right arm! Oh, it's in my right hand, like fire!"

"Halley-lou-yah!" the crowd cried.

"It's flowing into his head! Oh, how strong it is— like fire!—And it's healing him, healing him!"

. . . Stillness, absolute, deep; so still that Jack heard Mr. Ferguson's pocket watch ticking, and then Traveling Man was speaking again . . .

"Son, you have felt the power of God. Your head is healed!"

The boy nodded. His eyes, like two blubbers of foam floating on top of the milk bucket, were zeroed in on the preacher's.

"Now tell *them* what your name is," Traveling Man commanded.

"Huck Stevens."

The youth's words were clear, though his voice was high-pitched.

Mama O'Neal turned, looked at Mr. Ferguson triumphantly. "You still think he's a fake?" she asked.

"He ain't nothing compared to them snake handlers up around Forked Creek, Tennessee," Mr. Ferguson returned.

Jack remembered later that night that he'd snatched Peggy Jo's thumb out of her mouth. Under any kind of emotional strain, she always sucked it.

"Oh, that pore boy!" Peggy Jo whimpered.

Right after she spoke, Peggy Jo fell into Jack's arms in a dead faint.

It was after midnight before the doctor finished up examining Peggy Jo, who was then lying on her cot in the back of the tent, her eyes closed. Jack had gone back to town for the aging general practitioner soon after they'd come from the revival, because Peggy Jo had vomited twice on the road home; again, when she'd stepped out of the cab of the old flatbed truck.

"Just keep her in bed for a few days," the old doctor ordered. "It's nothing serious." Dr. McCauley, now eighty, knew very little about psychosomatic disorders, though when it came to treating strep throat, summer stomach upsets, flu and "fevers," he was competent enough.

Jack paid the modest fee to the old doctor, which was too much, considering what he'd done for Peggy Jo, then ushered him past the tree where Roosevelt was chained and stood in the dark until the taillights of the doctor's car disappeared in the night.

As he went inside, he was thinking that the five dollars he'd paid out wasn't much, still it would mean that this would be one week he couldn't send Colonel House a penny.

Peggy Jo's eyes were open, looking at him, as he crossed to his cot. "How you feeling?" he asked, making his voice deliberately gruff.

"Purty good," she answered. She sighed, then continued: "Well, one good thing, I won't have to climb no ladders tomorrow."

Chapter 8

"Sompin' big is gonna happen for sure, folks!" Mr. Ferguson said to Jack and Mrs. O'Neal. He clambered up one more step on the ladder to reach a cluster of peaches on a high limb, stood swaying dangerously for a moment, his legs like a drawn bow. "An-ser, a cold wind in August will bring hit! I don't know why, but hit will."

"You better come down from up there and let me pick the high ones!" Jack warned.

"Foot, boy, I got snow on the mountain, but I got a lot fire left in these here valleys of my body!"

Just then, the stepladder lurched sideways, and for a moment, the old Texan seemed to hang there in midair like a jump-shot artist shooting a basketball goal, then he came down heavily into the soft earth, landing on his sitter and back.

"Watch out!" Mama O'Neal yelled. "Watch out, there!"

Jack sprang to the ground and ran over to the fallen man, knelt beside him. "You all right?" he said, anxiously.

"Sure I am!" he said angrily. "Now git on back to work and mind your own business!"

But after Jack had gone, Mr. Ferguson lay there for a long time, his eyes peering up at the hard blue sky. A cool wind sighed in the pines along one side of the mountain, then rushed into the valley, stirring up dust.

At last Mr. Ferguson got up, and went back to his stepladder, walking stiffly. "Hit's that cold wind here in August!" he muttered. "Usually, I'm as surefooted as a mountain goat. No good ever comes from a cold wind in August, an-ser, we'll hear more about hit! Bad luck will come, or at least, bad news, as sure as dinnertime will!"

Jack had moved his stepladder to where he could reach the high cluster of peaches. Mr. Ferguson didn't say anything about it, but meekly picked from the lower branches. At last, he said:

"Now ain't it a pretty come-off, when a man gits so old he has to step down to a young squirt?"

Jack didn't answer him, for he knew that the time had come already when the old Texan would either have to give up fiddlefooting, else align himself with someone young and lithe who could pick the peaches (and later the apples) from the high branches. In considering his relationship with the old man, Jack realized that Mr. Ferguson had taken the place of his father in some ways. For one thing, Jack would never forget the way he'd saved Roosevelt from getting choked to death! He'd carry the load for him. He'd pick the high branches.

Of course, the Mexicans now went out of their way to be nice to Roosevelt, for the word had spread among them, not only the ones who'd chopped in the Delta City area, but the new bands who'd come from other parts of the country to pick peaches in the Ozarks. Quite often the men and their children would come up to the tent to stand and admire Roosevelt and feed him scraps of hamburger meat, and since Jack had to keep him chained, he was growing fat.

The cool wind kept blowing all morning, driving across the valley where the pickers were filling the baskets, and even though the dust got up with the wind, blowing into the pickers' eyes, ears, noses, and filming their lips so that when they licked them, grit was there, it was a cheerful crowd who sat down in the grass and choked down sandwiches of Treet, cheese and bologna.

"Why I didn't even get water but once," Mr. Ferguson said. He was sprawled out in the grass, digging the heels of boots into the rocky earth, eyeing Jack. "Hey, boy! You look plumb clean! An-ser, your shirt is as dry as my bandanner!"

Only two years ago Jack had been sensitive about not sweating. He was afraid that other choppers and pickers would think he'd been loafing. Once, he'd poured a jug of water down his chest and belly so that he would come in to lunch as wet as the others, but this past fall he'd begun to sweat more like a man did, and now his face didn't burn so turkey-wattle red, making the scar where he'd gashed his head run raggedly and angrily into his maverick locks.

"I bet you I made four dollars this morning," Jack finally answered. "I wish the weather would stay like this the rest of the summer."

Mr. Ferguson was shaking his head. "No good will come of this," he said, a note of warning to his voice. "I never did see a cold wind in August bring anything but bad luck."

Mama O'Neal made no comment. She lay back on the grass gazing off into the distance. A whirlwind got up farther down the valley, picked up force, and danced across the great peach orchard, skimming the ground, sucking up loose dirt and leaves, then lost its power in the branches of a large peach tree, making it roar and shudder for a moment, showering down dead twigs and overripe peaches.

" 'Fraid it's going to be a long dry spell," Mr. Ferguson mused, as he watched the whirlwind die in the orchard. "Picking cotton won't be no good this fall . . . little bitty bolls, and them not half opened."

Mama O'Neal still didn't make any comment. But she'd been this way since his father had died. He knew what it was, for he'd awakened more than once way over in the fag end of night and had heard her muted sobs. Jack still missed him, too. Lord, how he did miss him! But now he didn't listen for his words, his steps—the scraf-scraf of the gum-rubber boots in the dewy grass early in the morning, like he did those first weeks.

And yet there was someone he did miss, greatly. Irish O'Bannion! Not in the same way that he'd missed his father. The scene of the funeral in the Truxno-Graveyard had a finality to it, like the last word of a book. But Irish lived!—Lived!

"Time to grab a root and growl!" the old Texan boomed, sitting up stiffly, then pulling off his boots to knock the dust out of them.

"Man, this feels so good lying here in the grass, I'm a good mind not to get up!" Jack returned.

Several of the Mexicans had already taken their baskets and had started to work again.

"Sometimes I wonder what it is that makes a man keep on going," Mr. Ferguson said. "Now any sensible fellow would want to take his fishing pole and go down to the river this evening. An-ser, I wonder what it is that keeps him from going? What is it that keeps him answering the whistle?"

"Debts," Jack returned, thinking about the note Colonel House held.

"Maybe it is. Way back, I remember talking to a man who admired John L. Sullivan so much he followed him around all over the country. One time he said he asked him, 'John L., how did you get to be heavyweight champion of the world?' Right quick, Sullivan says, 'Because I got up and fought another round!' "

Mama O'Neal was then tying the big white scarf she wore securely about her neck. Jack walked across the orchard and selected four empty baskets, and as he crossed to the unpicked trees, he saw the old Texan stand up in the grass, heard his mellow voice, singing:

115

"Oh, it was in my heart like a melody,
Song of Old Sanantone—uh . . .
Lips so sweet and tender,
Like petals torn apart . . ."

He suddenly broke off his singing, walked into the sun and wind. "Mama told me there was gonna be days like this, and I didn't believe her!" he boomed. "Sanantone Rose! An-ser, wisht I was back in Texas this evening. Ain't gonna travel these old roads forever!"

Jack was thinking the same thing, as he plucked the tender peaches and dropped them into the basket.

Nanny Bell was gone! Peggy Jo told the news as soon as Mama O'Neal and Jack entered the tent. She was sitting up on the cot, her eyes red from weeping, and as she told about finding the goat missing, she began crying once more.

"I got up and went to the front to see what Roosevelt was barking at, and Nanny Bell was done gone!" she sobbed. "Done gone, not even her rope left!"

"Did you hear a truck or anything?" Jack asked.

"Naw."

"I bet you somebody is counting on a big barbecue!" Mama O'Neal said, wearily. "I bet you . . ."

"Oh, Mama!" Peggy shrieked. "Don't say that!"

"Well, a body has got to learn to face facts, girl!"
Mama answered. "What else would anybody want
with a blamed goat except to eat it!"

"I want Nanny Bell! I want Nanny Bell!" Peggy
Jo sobbed. And then, "Poor little thing!"

Mama O'Neal, seeing how her daughter was bucking and rearing on the cot, looked at her son anxiously.
"I reckon you better go and see if you can find her,"
she said. "At least try."

"All right." Glumly.

Jack went outside at once. Inquiring at several tents
and trucks, he always got the same answer from the
Mexicans. "No, señor. I have not seen your goat."

It was then that he remembered Mr. Ferguson once
worked on a ranch in Wyoming. He'd probably know
how to trail the goat, if she did break loose from the
tree and go off on her own.

On reaching the battered car parked far back from
the camp in the shade of a red oak tree, Jack saw
Mr. Ferguson lying down on a pallet reading yesterday's newspaper.

"Well, what brings you here?" he boomed, folding
the paper as he spoke.

Jack told him.

"Yeah! Second piece of bad luck that cold wind
of August has blowed us today!"

"Reckon could you trail her, if she went off herself?"
Jack asked.

"Reckon can I trail her . . .?" and he began to laugh.
"Can a hound-dog trail a rabbit?"

"I reckon she went back in those mountains . . ." and Jack pointed toward the hazy peaks rising up in the late evening sun.

"Yeah. And there's mountain lions there, too!" Mr. Ferguson said. "Last year when I picked down below the ridge, yonder, a fellow by the name of Blair come to town showing a yearling calf that had got chawed up and slobbered on."

"Well, if it just wasn't for Peggy Jo, I wouldn't ask you to help me, but you know how nervous she is, anyhow . . ."

"Of course, I'll help you!" he snapped. "More than likely, she's just grazed off somers. A blamed goat can climb a five-strand barb-wire fence! Why, hit can walk a sweet gum log rimed with ice across a raging creek! The Lord God-Almighty might have made goats and mules, but hit was the devil who give 'um their ways!"

The sun was yet warm on the slopes and brilliant in the branches of the evergreens on the mountains when Jack, Mr. Ferguson, and Roosevelt set out, following (so the old Texan said) Nanny Bell's footprints in the rocky soil. The trail led across the valley up the slopes into the mountains. Oak, cedar and blackjack were now thick, the grass deep and tender, the briers like barb-wire entanglements of World War Two, as they went into that land—past the abandoned shacks and cabins, with their pitiful outhouses rotting and falling in, and the smokehouse of logs, with the door standing open and letting out even yet an odor of the briny middlings and hams which had hung from bear-grass strips to the rafters. Gone, gone, in a mad rush to the towns and cities of the state, or pulling out for California, or Chicago, thinking those long, long thoughts, even as the migrants thought them; of the future time when they'd come back home again—home to the cabin, to the mountain, to the familiar haunts of squirrels and coons and bucks. But old man poverty had set up his tent in this land. They'd never come back, all of the old mountain-stock people. Already wilderness had reclaimed the land.

Rushing and scurrying through the grass, Roosevelt must have explored every side trail as they ascended the mountain. Once, a rabbit got up in front of him. He gave chase, barking eagerly, but soon lost the quivering bundle of brown fur in the high weeds. He came back to Jack panting hard, for he was now too fat, tried to spring into his arms, but Jack shouted him down.

"I declare, that dog just don't have no nose!" Mr. Ferguson lamented. "He couldn't trail a hot-buttered biscuit!" And then, seeing the hurt look on Jack's face: "But he ain't cut out for a trailing dog. He's good at what he can do, fighting and all. An-ser, they tell me that they make the best kind of seeing-eye dogs for blind folks."

"You still seeing some signs?" Jack asked.

Jack doubted that the old man was following any kind of trail. It seemed to Jack that they were taking a wild-goose chase across the almost endless stretch of mountain range.

"Here and there," Mr. Ferguson returned. "Just here and there. I figure she got loose right after we went to the field early this morning. Could be she's ready for having another little goat."

Later, he stopped on a little mesa and pointed out where the grass had been cropped. "See there," he said. "And if you'll look close, you can see her little hoofprint."

"For all I know that is a track of a deer," Jack said, gloomily.

The sun had gone. Purple shadows settled upon the valleys and turned faraway peaks into wavering gold-capped vistas of beauty. Jack knew that even if they started back to the camp right then, they'd have to walk most of the way in darkness. He remembered tales he'd heard of hunters getting rattlesnake-bitten in remote mountains like these, and how they'd died before they could get back to a doctor. But, so far, they hadn't seen nor heard of a snake of any kind.

As they crossed a narrow gulch, Mr. Ferguson saw the way Jack shied away from a gnarled root sticking out of the harsh earth.

"Why, you're jittery as a once-rode filly!" he chuckled. "I always say, let the snakes look out for themselves, and I'll look out for mine."

Jack noted the way the old man was breathing hard and fast; the way his shirt stuck to his gaunt shoulders. Something told him they'd better turn back, but he kept thinking about the way Peggy Jo had cried over Nanny Bell being lost. She loved the goat. Jack did, too, for somehow he associated the nanny goat with his father. She had given him life, hope, for a little time . . . the milk made mysteriously in her trembling body, and stored in her turgid yellow bag.

So they went on, down into gulches, then ascending to the opposite banks, until dusk dark came, and Jack turned on the lantern.

Passing down a bushy slope, suddenly, there was a little threshing sound ahead of them, then the mellow thumping of feet in the hard earth.

"Shine your light around that way!" Mr. Ferguson commanded.

He was holding the huge .45 in one hand. It looked as big as a Civil War cannon.

Jack moved the light around, as they walked. Then there was something—something ghastly and still—lying there in the rocky earth. A few more steps, and they were both staring at the remains of Nanny Bell, half-eaten, her entrails chewed where they bulged raggedly out of her ripped belly, but her head intact, with the leather belt holding the bell intact, and the rope around her neck. She had been mauled and slobbered on and her grizzled wool was clotted.

To keep Jack from crying, Mr. Ferguson solemnly *cussed* the varmint that did it. "Hit was a mountain lion! By Ganny, I'd like to look at hit over the sights of my six-gun!" he roared.

Jack, on the verge of tears, said desolately, "She ort to have had better sense!"

121

"Well, no doubt she was afeared," Mr. Ferguson mused. "But she was ready to have another little goat, and she was searching for an old billy goat, I reckon. That instinct is so blamed strong in animals that it outvotes all others! And that's the reason why it's so blamed dangerous, in man and beast."

"What will we tell Peggy Jo, though?" Jack asked.

"Now that is some problem," Mr. Ferguson mused. "Now us men can take such a sight as this, but I reckon now is the time for you and me to tell a few little lies."

"But if we don't bring her back . . ."

"Well, let's see—we can tell her we found her at this feller's cabin off up here in the mountains. We can tell her that this feller has nine young'uns, and he's down with an ulcer from eating so much fried sow-belly. We can tell her we just didn't have the heart to take Nanny Bell away from him, the way he was bedridden, and so pore you could see his heart a-beating like a little hummingbird's."

"And we could tell her that the man's young'uns was good to Nanny Bell and had combed her hair and had put a red ribbon on the bell strap," Jack said.

"Yeah, and that one little feller was toting her up some spring water to drink when we got there, and two more was out pulling her some grass and sweet gum leaves."

. . . They were going back, sticking to the high ridges, and avoiding the gulches as much as they could. Mr. Ferguson spoke of the time when they'd come back up here—some remote time in future. "We'll find that varmint," he promised. "He'll make a mighty purty decoration piece to hang in a man's room."

Jack was thinking about Peggy Jo, and how she'd take the news, all the way down the mountains, and when they came out into the clearing and approached the tent, he felt dread coil in his stomach.

As he came up to the entrance of the tent, he mentally rehearsed what he'd say to Peggy Jo, and he heard the voices of children inside.

Mama O'Neal saw him first. "Jack!" she said. And then, "Guess who's here?"

Chapter 9

Jack lounged by the tent entrance, thumbs hanging from his jeans pockets, making like he didn't even see Irish as she stepped toward him. "So this is the surprise," he mumbled.

"Of course, Jack! Run and hug her!" Mama O'Neal hissed. "Now act like a body orta act!"

Jack pretended that he didn't feel anything seeing her. She had changed her hairdo to an upsweep. It made her look taller.

She came up to Jack and grabbed his arm, shook it. "I don't believe that you're glad to see me!" she said.

And then her eyes filled with tears, as she looked up at him. He noticed that the blouse she wore was not so clean as the ones she always had on when she came to the field at Mr. Bob's plantation.

"Yeah, I'm glad to see you," he returned.

"Like I told yawl, he's been way back in them mountains," Mama O'Neal was saying to Mrs. O'Bannion. "I reckon he's about knocked."

Jack saw Mrs. O'Bannion sitting on one side of his cot. She had on nylons, but she was wearing low-heeled shoes. She looked pale, tired. Crowfeet lines rutted out from the corners of her eyes. He didn't see Mr. O'Bannion, as he stepped back that way to speak to her.

"'Lo, Jack," she smiled. And then, "I guess you think we've got the gall barging in on you like this."

"Nome."

"If you're wondering about her daddy, well—I can tell you! He left us. Just picked up one night and pulled out. Left us stranded out in a God-awful swamp—those mosquitoes, I'll swear they were as big as turkeys! And we stayed on and chopped until we had money enough to come here. I thought we'd pick along with you folks all the way up to the Missouri line, and with good luck, we can save enough money to get home on."

"Did you bring Nanny Bell in?" Peggy said in a small voice.

She was propped up on two pillows, eyeing him intently.

"Well, uh—I'll explain it all later, seeing we got company and all," Jack said quickly.

"No! I want to know now, Jack! Right now!"

"Goodness! Let him eat, dear," Mama O'Neal snapped.

"No, I want to know now!" Peggy Jo insisted.

Seeing there was no way out of it, he went into a long, rambling account of the night's adventure, spar-

126

ing no small detail. At first, he felt that he was not sounding convincing, and then, after he'd talked for a while, he got caught up in his own narrative, and told such heartrending whoppers about the poor family of mountaineers that Mama O'Neal and Mrs. O'Bannion began to cry.

"Oh, if you could have only seen that pore man lying there flat on his back; as pore as a cat living on lizards! And those cute little young'uns having to cut stovewood and slop the hogs and tote water from the spring! Oh, if you could have seen his wife wearing that flour-sack dress, and having to walk barefooted through briers to get to the pea patch. . . ."

"But I want my goat!" Peggy Jo said, whimpering up to cry.

"Now, don't you start bawling about that goat!" Mama O'Neal warned, wiping her eyes with the hem of her skirt. "You just think how bad your pore daddy needed that goat milk! We're glad to give hit to the fellow. And Jack did the right thing!"

"We'll just let him borrow her for a week," Peggy Jo said, hopefully.

"Nope. We've done give the goat away!" Mama snapped.

That settled it. Peggy Jo knew better than to cry about it. "A gal don't git too big to spank in my house," Mama O'Neal often reminded her.

"Jack, now come on and eat so you can go out to the tree and talk to Irish," Mama O'Neal said.

Jack was thinking about the way Nanny Bell lay

mauled and slobbered on in the rocky earth. "I'm not hungry yet," he answered.

Almost bashfully, he followed Irish out to the red oak tree. It was yet cool, but the wind that had been driving from the north all day had ceased. Stars dotted the sky. A full moon was getting up like a sunflower head in the east. They sat down beside each other.

"My, you can sure tell whoppers!" she said suddenly.

"How's that?"

"About the nanny goat. It wasn't the way you said it was, was it?"

"No. Me and Mr. Ferguson—we found Nanny Bell mauled to death, but I couldn't tell Peggy Jo that," he answered. "But how did you know I was lying?"

"I can just tell when anybody is lying, Jack. Daddy always could fool mother, but he couldn't me. Lately, he took to hanging out late at night in the juke joints. Lots of Sundays he'd tell mother he was going fishing. Instead, he'd go off with that old Webb man and get as drunk as a cooter. I told mother what he was doing, but she didn't believe me. I guess she just didn't want to believe me."

"How did yawl make out chopping, up the Arkansas Delta?" he asked.

"Old car stayed broke down half the time. Daddy stayed drunk all the time. I was very unhappy."

"The part of Arkansas I like best is Hot Springs. They got a sure crop down around there."

"What's that?"

"Tourists," he smiled. "That's a crop that don't require rain, sun, nor fertilizer."

"I want to go home," she said, sadly. "But there's just no work in the town since they closed down the mine."

"How come them to close it down?" Jack asked.

"Tennessee coal ain't hardly worth digging to begin with," she answered. "Everything was all right until the union people came in. The corporation claimed it just couldn't make a profit on the coal and pay the union scale, so they closed out, and the people had to move out, or get on the welfare."

"I want to save up money and buy me a little farm," he said. "I ain't wanting it close in to town, either . . . just close enough to a good road so that my young'uns can catch the school bus if I ever marry and have any young'uns."

"What about school, Jack?" Don't you want to finish high school?"

"Naw."

"Once a dropout, always a dropout, just like if you were on junk," she said.

"I ain't a dropout! I'm a migrant!" he said, angrily.

"What's the difference?"

"Well, a dropout just drops out of school and stays in the same community. A migrant only goes to school when he can't find work while he's in the community. I got most of my schooling in the early winter in southern Florida and south Louisiana."

Irish seemed to be talking to herself. "I was supposed to be Drum Major next year. Me and Louise Sistrunk were both after the honor. Well, just before school was out, Mr. Prentiss—he's our band director —called me aside one day and he says to me, 'Irish, I've finally made up my mind. You're the new Drum Major next year.' But I won't get it now. I was supposed to go to a clinic at the University of Mississippi and sharpen up, you know. It was held in June. I didn't have the money to go, but Louise Sistrunk's father owns a dairy. She went, so she'll be Drum Major next year, even if I do get back in school."

"It won't never be the same again, school won't," he said, sadly.

"Why, Jack?"

"You'll see! You'll be marked, like a beast, Irish. A fiddlefoot always is. It's a filth that soap won't wash off."

"Jack, don't be bitter! Don't give up! You've got just as much right to be in school as anyone else!"

Her face had lighted up, and she was very pretty, the way the moonlight accentuated the gold flecks in her eyes.

"You don't understand," he returned. "I got the rights. Everybody has, here in the United States, so this Mexican girl tells me. She lives down there—" and he pointed. "See where that truck is parked between the two big tents? Well, she lives in the one that's got the TV in it. Anyway, she studies history and civics and stuff like that all the time, because she's wanting to become a citizen. She's *allus* talking about what the law gives everybody, and all that. But I got news for her. Social acceptance don't come from laws, but from the hearts of human beings. She'll see. And you'll see."

"I'm going to finish my education!" she said, stubbornly. "Jack O'Neal, you just don't want to be anything but an old fiddlefoot! What do I care what the kids think?"

"You'll see," he said, glumly.

Later, they got up and walked down the road until they could hear the jukebox thrumming. The mountains were before them, towering and brooding. They talked of crops and places they'd been. Coming back toward the tent, he asked her if she'd like to go berry picking tomorrow evening.

"Yeah, I'd like that." Jack saw the sudden quickening of her breath. She tripped over a rock, and he shot out one hand and caught her before she fell. Her arm felt warm, soft.

"I thought all of the berries were gone," she said.

"All of the wild ones. Back in them mountains near the old homesteads tame ones were put out. I saw birds choking them down as we went up the eastern slope."

His heart was pounding when he thought some more about it. This time, Peggy Jo wouldn't have to tag along. She was down in bed . . . just me, and her —and Roosevelt, he thought.

As it turned out, Jack didn't get to go berry picking with her. In the orchard that morning, Mrs. O'Bannion spoke of home, and how she'd go there that morning if she had enough money for bus tickets. Mr. Ferguson heard her.

"By Ganny, I got just what you want!" he said. "I've been knowing Frank Lovelady and his woman, Mary, for right on to fo'teen years. You see, this time of year, he *allus* has a hankering to travel up to Maine and pick them big ole juicy apples. Of course I don't eat 'um anymore, because *they* put too much insect dope on stuff, and I figger anything that'll kill borers and bugs just might kill me, too. Well, Frank will go right through Memphis and on up through Tennessee clean in to Kentucky. I don't know exactly where yawl live, but Frank will take you there. He's got a heart as big as an eight-pound lard bucket."

"You aren't kidding me, are you?" Mrs. O'Bannion said, her face blushing with excitement.

"No, ma'am! This is serious business, when a body wants to git home! I got a hankering to see Texas again this fall, and I know how it is. An-ser, when dinnertime comes, if hit ever does"— and he looked at the sun—"I'll take you down the road there to where he's picking, and introduce you to him and his old lady."

"Oh, thank you, thank you!" she said, her voice breaking.

Irish was on her stepladder up ahead of them. She was better at picking peaches than she was at chopping.

"Irish!" Mrs. O'Bannion called. And she put down her hamper and ran across the dusty orchard until she came up to her. "Irish, baby! Oh, baby . . ."

Jack watched her as she told Irish the good news; saw the way Irish sprang off the ladder and ran to her mother and hugged and kissed her.

"Ain't it right pitiful, though!" Mr. Ferguson said, watching them carry on so. "Ain't they *flat* crying, though! Well, a womern sheds all kinds of tears. There's tears of happiness, tears of sadness, tears of anger, tears of disappointment, tears of jealousy, avarice, wickedness. In my time, boy, I've seen 'um shed all of them different kinds. But that's a womern for you. She ain't like us other critters. A womern is a collab job, son. One day, the Lord took the day off, and him and old Nick got together and kind of tried to see who could outdo the other; an-ser, the Lord done just as good as he possibly could!—He made her so pretty and dainty and nice that a body can hardly stand to look at her without falling down and worshipping her, and along come old Nick and did his part, just as good as he could, too. He made her cunning and jealous, and gave her the sure instincts of a wild goose, and last but not least, he give her tears. Hydrogen bombs can destroy the biggest city in the world, but a womern's tears can rebuild that city, and change up men where they won't want to set off no bomb."

All during the long two hours until dinnertime, Jack was hoping that something would happen to prevent Irish from leaving him for the second time, but as soon as the pickers called it a morning around twelve o'clock, Jack watched Mrs. O'Bannion and Irish walk across the ditch to where Mr. Ferguson had parked his ancient flivver.

They left in a cloud of light brown dust, with the engine of the old car coughing and wheezing, making the wheels lurch sideways, but this didn't bother Mr. Ferguson one whit. He'd often make fun of his own driving. "I druv hosses too long," he'd say. "And I drive a car just like a stuttering man talks."

Some twenty minutes later, after Jack and Mama O'Neal had finished eating and were lying stretched out in the cool grass, despite the chiggers, the old car came back in a cloud of dust, the same way it went off, and no sooner than it had come to a trembling stop at the ragged ditch, Irish slammed out and came running toward Jack, leaping the ditch as gracefully as a deer. "Going home! Going home!" she cried. "Oh, Jack, we're going home!"

At first he thought she was going to leap into his arms, but she checked herself in time, clung to one of his arms instead, and cried out in joy again, waving her free hand at the peach trees.

"Good-bye, ole hot sun and filth and fuzz!" she yelled. "Good-bye, Arkansas! Tennessee, here I come!"

Jack was like one struck dumb. "Ain't you gonna say anything!" she then cried. "Aren't you glad for me?"

"Yeah, I'm glad," he said dully.

134

He pulled his arm free and moved back from her, then added, "Now, you can Drum Major all you want to."

"You'll be leaving here soon, too," she said. "Maybe something will turn up for you, Jack. Maybe you can get back in school this fall."

"Naw," he said. "I ain't wanting to git back in it. I've had enough of being stared at like I was a circus freak, and giggled at, and ignored!"

"You've got an awful inferiority complex, Jack!" Angrily.

"You will, too, as soon as your classmates learn where you spent the summer!" he warned.

During the afternoon, Irish was quite gay. She had been so excited that she hadn't eaten more than two bites of the Treet sandwich she'd taken from the paper sack. At water breaks she'd sing and laugh and joke.

It seemed to Jack, as time drew near for her and her mother to leave the field (the Loveladys were leaving around four o'clock, but in order to finish loading their truck, they were quitting at two) that she kept trying to pick close to him, but he remained polite and silent, and answered her questions with "yeahs" and "naws."

Then Mr. Lovelady drove his truck along the meandering mountain road, and Mrs. O'Bannion saw him, took up her hamper and turned to Mama O'Neal. "Well, this is farewell, I guess," she said cheerfully, And then, coming over to where Mama O'Neal was picking, throwing her arms around her, embracing her: "Thanks for taking us in, honey!"

"I just hope you get a good job when you get home," Mama answered, stopping for a moment to fan herself with her old straw hat, her stiff finger standing out from her hand like a knot on a log.

"Bye, Jack, and thanks a million, Mr. Ferguson!" Mrs. O'Bannion crooned.

"Bye," Jack answered.

"Don't mention it," Mr. Ferguson grinned. Then he was whispering to Jack. "Go hug and kiss that sweet little Tommy good-bye, ignorant!—Go kiss her good-bye!"

"Naw."

"Jack . . ." Irish crooned, her voice trailing off. "Bye."

"Yeah," he mumbled.

She came to him, stood there as if she was waiting for something a moment, then seized his hands, wrung them, tears streaming from her eyes, and hurried after her mother.

"You fool!" the old Texan growled. "A body don't git to kiss a purty girl like she is every day in the week! What's the matter with you?"

Jack didn't reply; didn't look back toward the ditch where the truck was waiting for them. He heard their muffled voices, the sound of the engine being revved up as the truck moved back toward the road, but he didn't turn to look at it. But he smelled the dust of it, and as the dust settled on twig, leaf, and blades of grass, he began to pick like a madman, his eyelids batting back the hot tears.

Chapter 10

They journeyed north, now that September had come, following the apple orchards up through the Ozarks, the old trucks and fifth-hand cars in a rickety stream of traffic, meeting the cars and trucks pulling the house trailers en route to Miami, Florida, or Riverside, California. Many of the Mexican pickers had turned west, driving into Fort Smith, Arkansas, then south or southwest into the great Texas plains to pick cotton.

Mr. Ferguson loved the mountains in early autumn. Already oak, gum, and beech were reddening. The turtle doves sang no more in the valleys, and yet the grasshoppers gamboled in the dying grass, taking no thought, as the ant did, of the coming winter.

All of the days were the same to Jack, for in his mouth there was a taste of ashes, like it was during those first weeks after his father had died. He wouldn't think about Irish in the daytime, but at night she had a way of stealing into his dreams again and again. So he worked like an automaton, picking the apples that were rosy in color but of a poor quality, in shadow of torpid fall cloud, in sun, in shade, in rain and storm. He was sending Colonel House a money order each week now, sometimes with little notes attached, like:

DEAR COLONEL HOUSE,

This ain't much, just four dollars, but it's all I can spare this week. I reckon we'll be seeing you in a few weeks when the cotton opens up enough for a man to make some money picking. You ast about mama and Peggy Jo. They're purty good. Peggy Jo ain't puny no more, and mama has pulled out the new fall Sears Roebuck catalog and is looking at jackets and shoes and things. That's allus a good sign. So I guess we'll make it. Hoping to see you soon.

Yours sincerely,

JACK

The long, long fall rains set in while the little band of migrants were crossing southern Missouri, and that was when Mr. Ferguson got up one morning and stood outside the barracks they were staying in, looking at the gray clouds pushing slowly across the heavens. He saw Jack who'd come outside, too, and he began to shake his head. "I got a hankering to get back down on that Delta," he said. "Just because a body don't work, ain't no sign he don't eat!"

"Ain't but two Mexican families left out of our band," Jack answered. "And I heard Mr. Gomez say if it rained just one more day, he was pulling out for Louisiana."

"Let's git out from here!" Mr. Ferguson said, impulsively.

"When?"

"Right now!"

"Suits me. I'll speak to Mama."

Mama O'Neal was then standing in the door of the apartment. "I'm ready to start packing right now," she said.

"Grab a root and growl!" Mr. Ferguson boomed. "Hate to disappoint the boss man, but it's better that we go now while we still got money for gas than to wait until we have to sell our vehicles to have enough money for bread and beans!"

Later that morning Mr. Cheatwood came down from his fine brick home up on the hill the other side of the barracks, and stood out in front of the old cars and trucks, swelled up like a toad.

"What in the world has got into you folks?" he kept asking, as Mr. Ferguson walked back and forth to his car, carrying his knapsack, and "other pore trash" the way he put it.

"Time to go!" Mr. Ferguson muttered. "Time to go."

"How do you know?" Mr. Cheatwood cried.

"How does a wild goose know?" Mr. Ferguson returned.

"But, man!—God Almighty!—I got five hundred bushels of apples that's ready to pick!"

"Frost 'ull pick 'um for you." Mr. Ferguson said, cheerfully.

"Rakings and scrapings!" Mr. Cheatwood yelled, shaking one fist at the pickers. "No wonder you folks have got such a bad name!"

Mr. Ferguson didn't lose his head at this outburst, but looked Mr. Cheatwood in the eye and said, "The good Lord told that sick feller, 'Take up thy bed and walk.' Well, we're sick, too, Mr. Cheatwood . . . fevers and colds, and most of them little Mexican young'uns have got the trots. You know why? I think you do!— Hit's on account of the tadpoles and worms in the warter, the roaches near about as big as gators in the kitchen; so many rats they choose sides and play football amongst theirselves up in the ceiling every night!"

"You folks made me a promise!" Mr. Cheatwood stormed out.

"Reckon you must of fergot some of them you made us!" Mr. Ferguson snapped.

His old leathery face had reddened, and he kept clearing his throat, deep down, the way he did when he was mad.

Mr. Cheatwood began walking up the road, going back toward his house, strutting like a Plymouth Rock rooster. At the crest of the hill, he turned, looked back at the pickers. "Scum!" he yelled. "Filthy scum and offal!"

"Go away, *kiote!* Go away!" Mr. Ferguson bawled.

They had joined a big band of wetbacks picking cotton south of Lake Providence, Louisiana, in silent fields of cotton, white as a sea of alabaster. They had gone into that land, away from the Main Drag where the big cars rolled down from Memphis, heading for Florida; into that land where the one-room shacks of Negroes lay slugged by the sun, pitifully inept, with

140

a wringer-type washing machine sitting gaunt and battered on the bill-cap front porch, maybe side by side with an icebox fifth-handed out of a secondhand store, and Granny asleep in the rocking chair, with one rocker broken off, and the flies sitting and crawling on his face until it looked like a raisin cake . . . and if you stopped and spoke to him, he'd say, "Huh? What is it, folks? Why goodness me! It near 'bout sundown—got to quit dat taking them naps!" . . . on into that land, now going past the cabins, spaced some one hundred yards apart, abandoned now, with the well bucket wedged in the well, and the black-tub washpot turned bottom sides up by wild hogs, or somebody's wandering young'uns; and with grass growing up through the cracks in the porch floor, and the windowpanes knocked out of the windows—and even the Sears Roebuck catalog nearly halfway out of the pane it had replaced . . . on into that land, past the silent fields of white, as silent as any snow-smoth-ered meadow on a December morning, until they came to the big spring where the deer hunters camped in November. Already tents had been pitched in the best places in the clearing, but at sundown, with shadows stealing over the flats, the tents were deserted except for two aged, embrowned, toothless old women who kept the pinto bean pot at low heat and spoke in high, cracking voices, if they spoke at all.

By the time the Mexican families began coming in from the fields in backfiring trucks and cars, Jack, with the help of Mr. Ferguson, had the tent pitched, the meager furniture set up inside it, and Roosevelt tied out under a bushy-topped gum tree. Hombres, mujers, and muchachos came in straggling groups to admire Roosevelt, who had now grown quite *gordo* (fat) from having been tied up all summer, and from having been fed scraps of meat by his Mexican admirers from Delta City, Mississippi, to Noel, Missouri.

Jack still marveled at the way the news of his dog's fight with the wild boar had traveled. These were wetbacks who'd recently come to the Delta from the Rio Grande Valley region, strangers, all of them, and yet they knew the story about Roosevelt saving the Mexican children from getting eaten by wild hogs.

"Perro es muy bonita!" they'd stand and whisper. *"Perro es muy grande!"*

Mr. Ferguson moved among the Mexicans and spoke to them in their native tongue and found out that pickers were scarce this fall, though quite a number of the wetbacks were staying in a nearby village, choosing a roach-roamed boardinghouse rather than the wild, open Delta. "Señor, you have to pick late to make four dollars," one gap-toothed hombre warned. "The cotton, she no open good."

"By Ganny, I knew how picking would be here this fall," Mr. Ferguson had boomed. "I wisht I was back in Texas."

"I wish I was on a rocket headed for the moon," Peggy said.

She was standing outside the entrance of the tent scratching the skeeter bites. Mama O'Neal was working inside the tent in sullen silence, like she always did after they'd moved. But Jack knew that later on tonight, when she'd had time to rest a little, she'd come to his cot with that sad, mysterious smile on her face and lay her harsh, work-hardened hands, which were yet gentle with love, on his head and say, "Good night, son."

That was enough—this reward of love—to keep him going next day.

About sunrise every morning during the cotton picking season, people began coming toward Delta Pine Farms, Inc., from all directions. They came (the colored) riding in battered trucks from twenty miles away, or walking through the fields, wading waist high through the rank grass in the wet, low places. They came in pairs, families, droves.

There were two thousand and eight hundred acres of cotton to gather, and the Delta Pine Farms, Inc., were paying two dollars per hundred, and furnishing the water. Even though most pickers liked to work for the big corporation, there were never the same people in the fields for two days in a row. A colored family would pick for two days, maybe, then stay at home on the third day to go fishing. Then there were the stragglers and drifters who needed quick money for hamburgers and cigarettes, and never stayed at the plantation more than a week. The foreman, a man with small, beady eyes and a lean, clever face, liked to hire the wetbacks, for they'd work cheap and were mostly dependable, though recently the Federal Government had stepped in and had passed regulations governing housing and pay.

But the local laborers resented the wetbacks; even the colored did. It was the wetbacks, coming from the remote region of Old Mexico and speaking a language the locals did not understand, who kept the price of picking and chopping down so low, they thought. A few times, there had been incidents, in which the wetbacks had been harassed and intimidated, but generally all people who get their living by the sweat of their brows are peace-loving, for sweating together makes brothers of men, no matter the color, race.

"Ain't no need to blame the wetbacks on account of the low price for picking," Mr. Ferguson often said, arguing with some of the local pickers.

"They work too cheap," came the reply.

"Well, you know what will happen when and if we price ourselves any higher, folks! Why, the big boys 'ull just bring in the mechanical pickers—already doing it in most places anyhow!"

So the arguments ran, back and forth, as the people picked in the blowtorch-hot Delta sun until their backs gave out and they had to drop to their knees and crawl along, pulling their heavy ducking sacks.

On the third day, Jack's fingers, where they had been pricked by the burrs, began to bleed. Mr. Ferguson took adhesive tape from his knapsack and bound up Jack's fingers, and he kept picking.

Peggy Jo complained of having the fantods all the time. Quite often, she would balk on picking—would just sit down on her sack and stare at the hard, blue early October sky.

"Come on, gal!" Mama O'Neal would cry when she happened to look around and see her. "Put sompin' in that sack!"

Mr. Ferguson would shout words of encouragement to Peggy Jo. "It ain't long till dinnertime now!" he'd bawl. "I think I hear that bell dingdonging now!"

"But I'm tard!" Peggy Jo would whimper.

"Yeah? So am I," Mr. Ferguson would boom. And then, staring out into the sea of whiteness, "Mama tole me there was gonna be days like this! Hard times, son, she tole me. But I didn't believe her. But I was eating my white bread and didn't know it! Hah, hah!"

After a brief silence, then came the inevitable song, "Sanantone Rose" . . .

"Oh, it was in my heart like a melodee . . .
    Song of Old Sanantone . . .
    Lips so sweet and tender, like petals torn apart . . ."

"Jack! Jack!" Mama O'Neal called excitedly from inside the tent.

Jack went running. Mama O'Neal had rushed from the old truck like she always did, when they came from the field at sundown. There was supper to cook, breakfast dishes to wash, and holes that had to be sewn up in socks, jeans and underwear. He had loitered in the cool, gentle breeze for a moment, listening to Mr. Ferguson finish up a long-winded tale about a wolf hunt he'd been on in the Rocky Mountains, and when he heard his mother's cries he thought that Peggy Jo might have passed out again, for she'd complained of the heat all day long.

He sprinted through the entrance of the tent, held up quickly to keep from running over Mama O'Neal, who was walking excitedly about the tent, her stiff finger pointing in one direction and her good index finger pointing at the mess in the tent. Vaguely, he saw Peggy Jo crouched down on the broken remains of her cot, sobbing fitfully.

"Just look a-here!" Mama O'Neal cried. "Just look at this mess!"

The inside of the tent looked like it had been overrun by a herd of wild hogs, or that some latter-day General Sherman had made a march through the tent, cutting and hacking. The ladder-backed chairs were broken to bits, the cots lay in crushed heaps of torn sheets and with cotton leaking out of mattresses and feathers puffing out of pillows; the homemade eating table was caved in at the middle, so that it looked like a swaybacked horse, and the field stove had been smashed to broken slabs of metal, dishes had been knocked off the apple-crate shelf, glasses lay shattered near the dishes, the flour bucket had been crushed, the sugar container was lying bottom side up, the coffeepot had been knocked over, and this morning's grounds had oozed out the spout.

"Wild hogs!" Jack yelled.

"Even wild hogs can't climb up on shelves!" Mama snapped.

"Roosevelt wouldn't have let them hogs come in here, anyway," Jack answered.

"Well, where is Roosevelt?" Peggy Jo said, suddenly.

"That's right, where is he?" Jack cried.

A feeling of great dread shot through him. He'd been chaining the overeager dog inside the entrance for two days now. That was the only way he knew to keep the Mexican children from feeding him. Mr. Ferguson had warned Jack. "Them boxers die of heart attacks just like fat men do," he said. "And a body can tell Roosevelt is too blamed fat! Why, he's got fat-enfolded eyes like a meat hog!"

Just then, there was a sound outside the tent. A woman called in a high, cracking voice: "Señora! Señora!"

All three of them rushed out to see the two old Mexican women standing at the entrance. "Your dog, señor! Men come here in beeg cars. They had many dogs een them. They saw your dog and asked us what we would sell heem for. We told him, señor, that eet ees not our dog!" one woman said.

"They took heem, señor! Oh, eet was an awful fight!" the other old woman cried.

"But why? Why?" Jack asked.

"For the fights, señor!"

"What fights?" Jack asked.

"Don't know," she wailed. "They spoke of eet. Beeg dogfights, they said. Your perro, heem will make a good fighter! I heard one say."

"Dogfights? I ain't never heard of nothing but rooster fights!" Mama O'Neal said.

At times, while in the remote regions of the South, the wetbacks would hide out and fight cockerels they'd bought in the countryside, and bet on them. But Jack had never heard of fighting dogs except in one place in Louisiana.

"Which way did the cars go?" Jack asked.

"That way, señor . . ." and she pointed back toward the Mississippi River. "Beeg fights, they said. Your dog weel make much money, they said."

"Thanks," he said, in a terrible voice. And then, looking at his mother, "Mama, I'm taking the shotgun."

"Taking it where!" she demanded.

"I'm going after my dog!"

"You're not going nowhere, Jack O'Neal! Them men are dangerous!"

"I'm going after my dog!"

"Jack, don't you give me no jaw! You're mighty big to spank, but remember, I'm still your mama!"

"They took Roosevelt, and I aim to get him back!" he breathed.

"Well, if you want to go look for him, all right, but you can't take no shotgun! You find them men, and come back, and I'll sic the sheriff on them!"

Jack was already going out to the truck, as the two aged women went back to their pinto beans. Then Mama O'Neal was running like a fat hog toward Mr. Ferguson's flivver, calling, "Mr. Ferguson! Mr. Ferguson, come here!"

As Jack came up to the cab of the truck, Mr. Ferguson tossed down an old newspaper, stood up and faced Mrs. O'Neal.

"What's all of this tarryhooting around about?" he wanted to know.

She told him as quickly as she could. "I want you to go along with him and keep him out of bad trouble," she begged. "He ain't nothing but a yearling boy nohow."

"Just let me get my six-gun," he answered. And seeing Jack working with the switch of the truck, "Hold up there, young'un! I'm coming!"

Chapter 11

The first house Jack stopped at to inquire of the whereabouts of the dogfights was one of gray-weathered unplaned lumber, with two rooms on each side of a wide hallway, and a long, rambling porch at the front. It had been covered with cypress shingles (boards) but in places across the top, Jack saw where they had rotted away, and now in the late evening bats flew steadily in and out through the dark holes.

"Hello!" Jack called, as he walked toward the porch. "Hello!"

Not a sound. He saw last winter's wood yet piled on one end of the porch near the water shelf with the tin bucket and rusty long-handled dipper in it. Suddenly an old yellow cat came creeping up the hallway with gaited, synchronized steps.

"Don't look like there's nobody to home," Mr. Ferguson said. And then, "Aint that a pore make-out of a house, though!"

"Yeah, look at them rotten spots on the floor!" Jack answered. "When it rains, it pours!"

Suddenly there was a loud, terrifying groan from behind a thicket of pine and oak. Jack turned around and saw the corncrib, with the rail fence snaking around it. Then someone yelled, "Hold still, you old heifer!"

"There's someone down at the crib," Jack said.

"I'll get out and come with you," Mr. Ferguson answered. "Old knees are feeling stiff anyhow."

As they crossed to the crib, Jack saw a man dressed in overalls, blue shirt, and straw hat, struggling with a cow. A woman stood off a little ways. She had on a sloppy-looking print dress and a cloth bonnet, but she was barefooted. Her feet looked hard, leathery.

"Hello, folks!" Mr. Ferguson boomed.

He was then looking at the cow. Her belly, or at least some one of her bellies (cows have three), or from the way she looked, *all* of her bellies, were swollen tight as a bull drum!

The man looked around. He was trying to get a quart wine bottle into one side of the cow's mouth, but the cow kept turning her head sideways and lowing softly. Her breath came smothery and fast.

"Looks like you got a sick cow!" the old Texan boomed.

"Hidy."

The man spoke in a dead flat voice through his long nose.

"Soloman, maybe these fellers knows a heap about sick cows," the woman said in a shrill voice.

"Old fool got in the pea patch and et up all of my dried peas," the man said, as if his wife hadn't spoken. "Now, she's swole up, and my name is Soloman Snipes, and that's my womern," and he pointed at her, "Eula Lee."

"Right glad to know you!" the old Texan boomed. And told his name and Jack's.

"Soloman, that cow is gonna bust right here!" Eula Lee warned.

"She'll just have to bust!" Soloman snapped.

"Good Lord! This ain't nothing!" Mr. Ferguson boomed. "Why, when I was back in Texas working on the old Bar X Ranch, I had cases like this all the time!"

"Yeah? Well, I been trying to drench her with salts, but the old fool don't have sense enough to know I'm trying to help her," he twanged.

"Drenching ain't gonna git the job done, not a-tall!" the old Texan answered. "Ain't but one thing you can do to save her now, and that's to operate."

"Operate?" Eula Lee questioned.

"Yeah. Let me see if my pocket knife is sharp enough," Mr. Ferguson returned, reaching in one back pocket and bringing his jackknife out.

He tested it on his thumb. "Hit's sharp enough. Mostly, I'll be stabbing anyhow," he said.

"Soloman, don't let him kill our milk cow," Eula Lee said, peering at Mr. Ferguson intently. "Why, milk and butter is all we've got to eat, now that old Sooky has et up the cowpeas."

"Hit ain't no matter if she did eat up them cowpeas," her husband twanged. "I done et so many of them now that I dread going past the pea patch."

153

"Jack, you come and help Soloman here," the old Texan directed. "We've got to throw her down to operate. On the other hand, the way she's swole up, a body would have a time holding her down. Look the way her legs seem to stick out of her sides!"

"Soloman, don't let him kill our cow!" Eula Lee said.

"Madam, your cow is gonna die anyhow if sompin' ain't done!" Mr. Ferguson snapped. "Listen at her breathing, would you! And look the way her eyes are walled."

It took some rassling around to throw old Sooky down. She finally sort of keeled over, groaning painfully, then sticking out one hind foot, Jack saw, as he held on to her head.

Mr. Ferguson had knelt beside the swollen belly, his knife held ready. Old Sooky let out a low groan. "I wish I had a trocar," the old Texan said.

"What's a trocar?" Jack asked.

"Ah, it's an instrument just for this kind of operation," Mr. Ferguson said. "It keeps the incision open where the gas can escape. But this knife will do the job. Now, hold her steady, boys . . ."

"Don't you kill my milk cow!" Eula Lee warned.

She saw the knife upraised, turned her head, and stepped over to a fence corner.

Jack saw the knife descending into the distended belly, felt Sooky flinch as the point stabbed into the belly, heard the eructions of escaping gas. Then Sooky began groaning again, but not with pain. Her relief was almost instantaneous. Soon, her breathing returned to normal, and she looked normal out of her eyes.

"Let her up, boys," Mr. Ferguson said.

"Is she healed already?" Eula Lee said, anxiously.

"Old heifer is feeling fine," Mr. Ferguson drawled. "An-ser, give her another thirty minutes, and I bet you she gives down her milk."

The cow kind of quivered a little, then sidled off toward the crib, her hocks snapping like stepped-on dried butter beans.

"Mister, I sho'ly thank you for healing my cow!" Eula Lee said.

Eula Lee was watching the cow closely. It seemed that old Sooky was ready to eat some cottonseed meal and hulls. She stood at the door of the crib mooing softly.

"Why, that ain't no operation a-tall," Mr. Ferguson said. "I reckon I must have performed it a hunnert times in my life."

In a little, Jack asked about the dogfights. "We hear they have dogfights around this neck of the woods," he said.

"I don't keep dogs," Soloman said. "Yeah, I've *heered* tell of the dogfights. I've seen all of them big cars with out-of-state tags on them, and I've seen the dog crates. Hit's up toward the river some," and he pointed toward the bottom.

Jack thanked him and he and Mr. Ferguson started walking back to the truck.

155

"Now what I can't figure—how did them peckerwoods learn about Roosevelt being such a good fighter!" Mr. Ferguson said.

"It's known from here clean to the Canadian border!" Jack answered. "The wetbacks spread it everywhere, but I don't think any of them would have told whoever it was where they could find my dog."

"Naw."

"But they have to hide out to hold the fights," Jack said. "I reckon it's against the law."

"Yeah, it's against the law, and so is making whiskey, but there's a heap of stills around," Mr. Ferguson said.

Just as they came to the truck, Soloman gave out a yell. "Just a minute," he called. "Maybe I can help you some more."

He came across the weed patch, his feet going swish-swish as he stepped. His face was pleasant enough now that he'd decided his milk cow was going to live, though the short, bristly beard gave it a dark cast, like a corpse Jack had once seen that hadn't been embalmed.

"Me and the old lady been talking hit over," he grinned. "I reckon I ain't told all I knowed about them dogfights. I know all about hit. Dogfighters from twenty states done begin to come into these diggings. They got them special-trained fighting dogs, and they git here a day or two before the fight fans and gamblers, mostly."

Jack felt queasy. Roosevelt fighting a wild boar that didn't have anything but his tusks and instincts was one thing; fighting a special-trained killer dog was another!

"Let's get going! You can tell us on the road," Jack said, quickly.

"Now, I ain't a-wanting them gamblers coming after me!" Soloman said, uneasily.

"We'll take care of the gamblers!" Mr. Ferguson said. "I got my six-gun in that dash, there."

"Well, if you're certain about hit!" Soloman answered.

"Get in!" Jack said, impatiently.

As the truck eased along the dirt road in low gear, Jack saw car tracks that looked fresh. He mentioned that to Soloman.

"Some few come in this way, but most of them come in from south of here," he said. "I mean they got them a regular association, just like churches has. They call hit the National Dogfight Meet Association."

"Well, what kind of dogs do they fight?" Mr. Ferguson asked.

"Hit's a special bred dog—I heered them say the name of them—specially bred Staffordshire terriers, they called them," Soloman answered.

"You ever see 'um fight?" the old Texan asked.

The truck was then stroking down a deeply wooded road that snaked off into a land of shallow sloughs, foul, knee-deep lakes where wild rice grew.

"Yeah. I seed 'um. One time I was out hog hunting and I kept meeting them cars a-coming up from the highway, and I noticed that each one of the car trunks had air cracks, and a time or two I heered the dogs growling. Well, I figgered some bunch from town had come in here to hunt deer out of season—they do that, you know, though I'll tell you one thing, we got a game warden who is part Indian. I gar, he goes around through the bottom barefooted, and he ain't a-skeered to tangle with a circle saw! . . . Well I thought hit was a outlaw deer-hunting party, but when I seed one trunk come open—seed that hairy-mouthed dog—I knowed hit wasn't no deer-hunting dog, and so I sneaked through the woods till I come to the place where I'll show you. Hit's just like a boxing ring, with seats and all."

Jack saw the crossroads up ahead of them; saw the way the fresh car tracks had turned the earth to pumice, with a thin scuffing of brown on the sumac bushes that lined the shoulders of the road.

"Slow down some!" Soloman directed. "Better be looking for a place to park this tin heap. We'll have to walk through the woods some if we don't want to get *seed*."

Jack pulled over, crushing down bushes and vines, and parked the truck underneath an oak with low-sweeping limbs. They got out and waited for the swamp rat to show them the way.

Although it was not sundown yet, already it was getting dark in the bottom. Owls whoo-whooed off down a big slough. Frogs peeped in the ankle-deep water in front of them, and as they walked toward them, got up and went desperately leaping into the mossy bushes.

Jack was so busy watching where he put his feet that he was hardly aware of the way clouds of mosquitoes settled upon his back, shoulders, neck and arms, and as the three men slipped through the swamp they were slapped in the face by tree limbs, held by vines, and scratched by briers.

Suddenly Mr. Ferguson had stopped, was standing —leaning forward, cupping one ear.

"What's that?" he asked.

"Hit's them dogs growling!" Soloman answered. "It ain't far now."

They slipped right up close to the small arena, though they couldn't see anything but the big pen in front of it. Two men were in the pen, doing something. Jack couldn't tell what it was.

"Is the fight on?" Jack whispered.

"Nope, hit's over," Soloman said, hoarsely. "See that dead dog they're toting off!"

Jack craned his neck, but he couldn't see the dog.

"Many people there?" Jack asked.

"A big crowd of folks, hit looks like to me," Soloman answered.

Soloman had climbed upon a rotten log. He had a better view than did Jack or Mr. Ferguson. Suddenly there was a burst of loud talking, then someone was cursing in a foreign tongue.

159

"Are them Mexicans?" Jack heard Mr. Ferguson ask.

"Nope. Cajuns. I can see them," Soloman returned. "And you know they act plumb skeered or sompin' . . . keep looking back down that new-cleared road."

"Afeered the sheriff will come, and this here arena looks like a church house with just one door to me," Mr. Ferguson said.

"Let's get in closer!" Jack said.

He couldn't see anything now, but he heard the drone of voices, and the tinny sounds of beer cans being tossed into the bushes.

"Better stay down, son!" Soloman advised. "I figger them gambling men are dangerous. Hit looks like I see guns a-bulging out from their chest. I figger they're wearing shoulder holsters."

Mr. Ferguson was checking his .45. It looked shiny, almost new.

"They're turning on big lanterns and things," Soloman said. "Now, they're bringing in them long-haired dogs, with them great big white teeth! Hit looks like they come here to fight, too!"

"Are the long-haired ones fighting each other?" Jack asked anxiously.

"Yep. But I seen them bringing out a different-looking one," Soloman said.

Jack stepped closer to the arena, pushing back a black gum bush, but he couldn't see anything but the poles then.

"What does the new dog look like?" Jack asked.

"Well, hit looks like a bulldog in the head, but hit's got real long legs."

"What color is it?"

"Well, hit looks kind of roan-colored to me, with a white splash down hit's chest."

"That's Roosevelt!" Jack breathed. "I'm gonna go claim him!"

"Wait a minute!" Mr. Ferguson called.

But Jack was already pushing through the bushes, his face set in an angry mask.

"You fool! Come back here!" Mr. Ferguson hissed.

But Jack didn't stop. Ahead of him in the dim light, he saw the swart-faced man leading Roosevelt toward the pen.

Chapter 12

"Jack, wait!" Mr. Ferguson begged, desperately.

Jack looked around to see him threading through the thicket; saw the .45 he held in one hand. In front of him was the crude arena. Trees had been sawed down. Seats had been built of heavy bridge timber in a circle around the fighting pen. It looked something like the Greek theater Jack had seen at the University of Arkansas three summers ago when his family had been en route to Noel, Missouri, and had taken the wrong road out of Fayetteville.

Vaguely, Jack was aware that Mr. Ferguson was holding on to one of his arms with a steel-trap grip, as they stood in the shadows of the arena. Vaguely, he was aware of the noise; of the loud talk and beery laughter of the men, some seventy-five of them who sat on the crude seats; of the snarling dogs in the pen who were strangely not fighting each other, and of the snarls of his own dog which was held by the swart-faced man standing at the gate of the pen.

"Money is being passed!" Mr. Ferguson whispered.

"Yeah, but I'm going to claim my dog before that man puts him in the pen!" Jack answered.

"Now wait a minute, Jack! Soloman is done gone! Ain't but two of us against that whole crowd! As good a shot as I am, I don't like them kind of odds," Mr. Ferguson said.

Then the swart-faced man was waving his fat billfold in the air, holding on to Roosevelt's chain with the other hand.

"Anybody!" the swart-faced man said. "Just lay your money down! Even money that *my* dog kills both of them!"

Several men came out of the crowd's crush, their billfolds out. As Jack watched the money pass, it suddenly dawned on him what was fixing to happen. My Roosevelt is being matched against two hairy-mouthed fanged killers, he thought. They'll kill him, too, because Roosevelt ain't in shape like he was when he fought the wild boar! He had to do something, now!

Suddenly Jack wrenched his arm loose from the powerful fingers that encircled it, sprinted across the clearing, charged up to where the swart face was passing money. "You fool, you!" Mr. Ferguson bawled.

There was an astonished look on the swart face. Jack saw the hand with the billfold moving to a hip pocket. Jack reached out one hand, seized the chain. "Gimme my dog!" he commanded.

The swart-faced man put the billfold away, then shoved his freed hand into Jack's belly. "Back up, kid!" he snapped. "I'll slap the h— out of you!"

"I want my dog, you thief!" Jack breathed.

"Joe! Mooks! Come get him!" the swart-faced man yelled.

Then men in the crude bleachers had stopped laughing and talking. "What is this?" someone said anxiously.

"Who let this kid in?" the swart-faced man yelled. "Joe! Mooks! Where are you?"

Jack wasn't aware of the two men coming up behind him. "You stole my dog!" he cried. "I'm taking him home!"

"You're crazy, kid!" the swart-faced man said, with a cold laugh. "My name's Ledet—Henri Ledet. I raised this dog! I got the papers on him."

Jack felt the big hands bite into his shoulders, felt the chain tighten against his hands. Roosevelt whined nervously. He seemed to be confused by the noise and lights. Man had always been his friend, with but few exceptions. He didn't understand it.

"Take him away, boys, but don't hurt him!" Ledet said. Ain't nothing but a kid . . . thinks this boxer is his dog. Swamp rats ain't got much sense nohow."

The two men pulled Jack, kicking and screaming, toward the bleachers, then forced him down on a heavy bridge timber and held him there.

Jack was looking wildly about him. He saw the swart hand opening the gate to the small pen, heard the guttural snarls of the bearded dogs inside it—saw their long, white teeth, where their lips had peeled back over them.

"Mr. Ferguson!" he yelled. "Mr. Ferguson!"

There was no answer. Mr. Ferguson had deserted him. "Old windbag!" he panted. "Always bragging how good he can shoot, but when the showdown comes . . . !"

There was a roar from the crowd, but Jack couldn't look at the dog pen. He heard the snarls, growls, the snap-snap of striking teeth. Then some old-timer began talking excitedly. "I gad, I never did see no dog-fight like this'n before! Oh, ain't they laying aholt of one another, though! I mean that boxer *pintly* come here to fight! I gad, hit's nip and tuck! Hit's gonna be mighty hard to tell if them two Staffordshire's can *whump* that boxer! Oh, look at him! Look at him slash! Head's big as a cedar water bucket, ain't hit, fellers!"

There came an appreciative roar from the crowd, then the old-timer was yelling: "Look at that son-of-gun rear up on his hind legs and strike out with his forefeet! God Almighty! No wonder they call hit a boxer!"

Another roar from the crowd. "Uh, oh!" the old-timer bawled. "The big boxer's in trouble! Them two hairy dogs has got him down! Look at that, would you!"

Jack felt his heart come up in his throat . . . felt his head whirl crazily . . . heard the roar of the crowd, the growls of the dogs . . . smelled the stench of them, bigger than the odor of the funky-smelling swamp soil.

He couldn't look, but he had to look! He saw the tangle of threshing bodies under the hot lights of the pen, saw Roosevelt spring away, saw the way the white splash down his chest was splotched with crimson.

Jack couldn't stand it. He closed his eyes to the awful sight before him, but he couldn't close his ears, because the two men were holding his wrists, and watching the terrible fight all at the same time.

"The boxer is bleeding bad!" the old-timer yelled.

"The devil he is! That blood is from them other two dogs!" Ledet yelled. And then, "That's it, son! That's doing it! Come on, boy!"

"Look at the way he run right smack over that Staffordshire!" the old-timer hollered. "Look at him use his weight, would you! I gar, his head's as big as a cedar water bucket! I gar, hit looks like a tiger head, don't hit, boys!"

"Come on, boy!" Ledet yelled. "That's knocking him back! Come on, money-maker!"

"Look at them rear up would you!" the old-timer yelled. "Be blamed if I don't believe I'm gonna win some money! Blamed if I don't think that boxer can *whump* both of them other two!"

Jack got so excited that he took the dry heaves like a football player coming out of the dressing room just before kickoff. "Oh, me! Oh, me!" he moaned.

"Shut up, kid, and watch this fight!" one of the men said. "Heck, don't you like excitement?"

"That's my dog!" he heaved. "He stole my dog!"

"Shut up, kid!"

"Looky there! Looky there!" the old-timer bawled. "They got the boxer down again! Oh, he's in bad trouble now!"

Jack heard the terrible snarls, the vicious snap of strong teeth, then above these sounds, Ledet's curses. "D— you! Get up, boy! Roll, boy!"

"They're choking hit to death!" the old-timer yelled. "But look how that smaller Staffordshire is bleeding! Oh, look at hit . . . just bled down and keeled over like a stuck hog!"

"That's it, boy!" Ledet shouted. "Now, now!—Just one on one now!"

"That other Staffordshire is kilt!" the old-timer yelled. "Look at them two rear right straight up in the air, like two stud horses! Look at the slobber running out'n their mouths! God Almighty! Look at that boxer's teeth—like big fangs!"

"That's it, boy!" Ledet cried jubilantly. "Now, you've got him, boy!"

Jack felt weak, weak. He heard the growling, snapping, the sickening rip of teeth as they bit and slashed into exposed chest, flank, neck. Then the old-timer was yelling again.

"The boxer's got a good *holt* now! That's all she wrote, folks!"

Above the sound of Ledet's hoarse cries of triumph, Jack heard the men who'd evidently bet on the two Staffordshires stomping their feet on the heavy planking—heard their disgusted curses.

"I gar, I ain't never seen nothing like hit before!" the old-timer breathed. "That's the sixth dog he's kilt this e'nin'!"

Jack had to force himself to look at Roosevelt. He was standing at the gate of the pen, his tongue lolled out, breathing so fast it was hard to tell when he sucked in and spewed out. His head was specked with blood. One ear was torn raggedly, but it bled but little. The splash of white down his chest was now a splash of bright red.

Jack saw Ledet open the gate, saw him kneel beside the tired, hot dog, begin to run his fingers over his body.

In a few minutes he stood up, turned to the crowd, and said, "He's nicked in a few places . . . nothing serious. He'll be ready to fight again in thirty minutes."

"He's not fighting my dog!" someone said adamantly.

"Nor mine, either!" said another.

"I thought that's what we came here for!" Ledet snapped. "Okay. Pay me off, boys! I got the National Champion!"

"Like h— we are! He's got to fight that English bulldog first!" someone said angrily.

While the men formed little football huddles and argued among themselves, Ledet came to where Jack was held down and said, "Let him go, boys." He had several bills in one hand. He shoved them toward Jack. "Here, kid! Here's five hundred dollars! Take the money and go home, see!"

169

"My dog ain't for sale!" Jack laughed nervously. It sounded silly somehow.

Ledet shot out one hand, grabbed Jack's disheveled hair, pulled, twisted, until Jack winced with pain.

"You take this money, kid!" he commanded. "And I want you to take a good look at my face! I ain't a man known for his generosity! I'm offering you five hundred for the dog. He's worth every penny of it to me!"

"He ain't for sale!"

"Okay. Joe, you and Mooks take him down the road and head him out of the bottom. If he comes back, shoot him!" Ledet snapped.

Just as the men pulled Jack down from the bleachers, from far back in the darkness a voice called, "Here comes the law!"

"Everybody scatter!" Ledet yelled. "Get your dogs and head back to your cars through the woods!"

There was a mad scramble as the men rushed down from the bleachers and sprinted into the darkness of the swamp. Some forgot their dogs in their excitement. Some threw the crates down after they had struggled into the bushes.

Jack and Ledet went after Roosevelt at the same time. Ledet got to the pen first, opened the gate, grabbed Roosevelt's collar, and led him out. Jack met him there. He plunged into Ledet, knocking him back.

"Why, you little squirt!" Ledet raged, striking out at him.

The blow struck Jack's shoulder, knocking him back. Then Jack grabbed the hairy forearm, held on to it, sank his teeth into it. Ledet yelled with pain, and that was when Roosevelt nabbed him . . . sunk his teeth in one thick thigh. Ledet screamed, blindly kicked out at the dog, lost his footing and fell heavily into the tramped earth, with Roosevelt right on top of him, his teeth snapping at Ledet's throat.

"Get him off!" Ledet begged. "Grab him, please!"

"Come here, boy!" Jack yelled, seeing the way Roosevelt was trying for Ledet's throat. "Come back, sir!"

Just as Jack seized the leather collar, he heard a sound behind him. Then Mr. Ferguson, .45 in one hand, came into the golden circle of light. Behind him was a tall man in an olive-drab uniform.

"You're under arrest!" the uniformed man said to Ledet, who bucked and writhed on the tramped earth, holding on to his thigh.

"Just do something with that dog!" Ledet begged.

"I've got the dog!" Jack said, holding on to Roosevelt's collar with one hand, stroking his ragged coat with the other.

"The Humane Society agents will be right glad to see you," the game warden said. "They're looking for you folks all over south Mississippi and central Louisiana anyhow."

"But there's a lot more of them!" Jack said. "They ran through the woods with their dogs when they saw you coming."

"Yeah, we heard them—sounded like a hailstorm in a red oak thicket," Mr. Ferguson boomed. "That's the reason I left you and went in the old truck for help. I knowed there was just too many of them jokers."

"All of them others are getting away!" Jack said.

"They won't get far," the game warden drawled. He was a weather-browned man of thirty-odd, with a lazy smile that always hovered about his quiet face. He had one hand in his pocket. He brought out a handful of car keys. "Funny thing, how folks just won't bother to take these out."

Chapter 13

Jack decided that the only thing left to do was move on up the Delta to Colonel House's plantation and ask him for mercy. The tent furniture had been completely wrecked, and though Sheriff Bob Murphy had jailed Ledet and twenty-five of the other dog-fighters he'd caught, waiting to turn them over to Fred Meyers of the Humane Society, that still didn't bring back the furniture.

Mr. Ferguson was all for moving out of the Big Springs camp. He helped Jack load up the few remaining articles that hadn't been destroyed, and around nine o'clock that morning they started up the Delta, following the meandering levee. There was the smell of the mudbanks, fetid, hot, and the sight of the willow trees, their leaves curled up to the hot sun.

Around eleven o'clock, Jack sighted the antebellum mansion set back behind the forest of pecan trees, and he began slacking off some on the worn accelerator as he approached the turnoff.

He parked in the shade of a huge pecan tree, got out, and went in, leaving Mama O'Neal and Peggy Jo fanning themselves.

Mr. Ferguson, who'd parked his flivver right behind the truck, was reared back mopping his face with a soiled bandanna.

Colonel House was on the great back porch this morning waiting for lunch. He had on his gold-rimmed spectacles. He had been reading Horace, in Latin, though Jack didn't know that, as he watched him turn around in the rocking chair.

He acted like he was glad to see Jack. He got up and extended one rosy hand. "How do, son!" he said in a kind voice.

"Hidy," Jack blurted, his courage deserting him.

He had intended asking the aging man for a loan to buy new furniture, but somehow the words wouldn't come in his mouth.

They chatted for a time, with the Colonel's keen blue eyes zeroed in on Jack's face. Then the Colonel said, "Jack, I'm real proud of you! You've kept your courage up. Losing your father would have been a severe blow at any time, but coming when it did, you just being a lad-of-a-boy, I think you've really proved yourself. Now, I've got plenty of land. I often asked your father to settle down on some of it, but he wouldn't talk to me, but if you . . ."

"Colonel House, I come to borrow more money!" Jack blurted.

He felt his face burn, felt his hands begin to ooze moisture.

"Why's that, son?"

In a stumbling, halting manner, like a cow walking toward a dipping vat, Jack related what had happened to their belongings.

"You said it takes money to make money, Colonel," Jack ended up saying.

"You're absolutely right. Why, sure, I'll let you have the money. How much?"

"Well, I thought about an even hundred. I think that's about what I've paid back."

"You sure you won't need more? All hardware goods have gone up during the last ten years."

"I think we can make out on an even hundred."

"Very well. Let's go to my office."

. . . Ten minutes later, Jack was going back to the truck, with ten crisp ten-dollar bills clutched in one hand.

Mama O'Neal was smiling at him. "A body never knows how a young'un will turn out," she said. "Blamed if you ain't near about as good at borrowing money as your daddy was."

In a scant week's time, the pickers had finished up the cotton on Colonel House's plantation, and were moving daily up the Delta into Arkansas. But the cotton was light, the burrs unevenly opened, because of the long dry spell.

Each day, Mr. Ferguson bragged about how much better picking was in west Texas. "Why, hit's a heap cooler out there, and sometimes the cotton is a lot better," he said.

"I thought they used mostly mechanical pickers there," Jack returned.

Once, the O'Neal family had moved up the Texas Panhandle, but Jack's father hadn't liked the heat, the absence of trees, rivers, and lakes.

"If I'm happy, I've got to be where I can hear birds singing in trees, see green hills behind a hay meadow," he'd grumbled. "This here Texas—like living in one big gravel pit!"

"Well, they do use a lot of mechanical pickers," Mr. Ferguson mused. "But it's just like it is here in the Delta—a lot of folks don't."

"Well, one thing I like about this plantation here is the highway running right smack dab through it!" Mama spoke up, standing up straight to rest her back for a moment.

"And I like the barracks!" Peggy Jo said.

"Yeah, barracks do beat a tent, if it ain't got roaches," Mr. Ferguson answered, looking up at the hazy fall sky for a moment. "Now, I hate roaches with a purple passion! I wisht I had all of them in the world in a brown paper sack. I'd carry hit to White Plains, New Mexico, and let 'um set off one of them 'tomic bombs under hit!"

"I wish I had a big bowl of ice cream—as big as that stock pond in Mr. White's pasture!" Peggy Jo sighed.

Looking back toward the gray barracks at the end of the field, Jack said, "Come on now, Peg! It'll soon be quitting time. Maybe we can drive into town and go to the show tonight."

"Waaaaaaaaaaaaaa! Waaaaaaaaaaaaaaah! Waaaaaaaaaaaah!"

"Jack! Jack!" Peggy Jo called.

"Huh? Huh? he said, sitting up quickly in bed, one hand wiping sleep out of his eyes.

"Hear that! Hear that!" Peggy Jo said, her voice trembling.

Jack shook his head. He looked around him. It was yet dark outside. "Hear what?" he said.

"That! That!"

A rooster crowed way over toward the levee. A truck hummed over on the highway.

"Just a rooster, sissy baby!" Jack snapped. "Now go on back to bed! It ain't near daylight! I bet you one thing, I don't carry you to see one of them old horror pictures again!"

Especially since her father had died, Peggy Jo had been scared at night.

"Of what?" Mama O'Neal had often asked.

"Sompin' gonna git me!" Peggy Jo always sheepishly replied.

"Waaaaaaaaaaaaaaah! Waaaaaaaaaaaaah! Waaaaaaaaaaaah!"

Jack heard the sound. It rang a bell in his sleep-fogged brain. A baby's cry is unmistakable. Jack looked around to see his mother on her cot. She was sleeping with her mouth open, going puff-ahhhhhhhh

. . . puff-ahhhhhhhhhh. Quite often she sang spirituals in her sleep. She simply loved the Blackwood Quartet!

Suddenly Roosevelt began to bark hoarsely, and that was when Jack's feet jarred the floor. He swished on his jeans quickly, then soundlessly crossed to the door, eased it open, turned on the outside light. And this is what he saw:

A small brown-paper-wrapped bundle lay on the steps. It squirmed, stretched, closed its eyes to the light, and howled shrilly. Roosevelt, who'd been standing over the bundle, began to bark again.

"Shut up!" Jack called. "Git!"

And then he was calling excitedly, "Mama! Oh, Mama! Git up! Git up!"

"Ain't it a baby, Jack?" Peggy Jo yelled.

"Yeah, all wrinkled and red and it's got a flat-looking forehead like the picture of Charles Darwin —the one in my ninth-grade science book!"

"What in the world is going on?" Mrs. O'Neal said, thickly.

Jack heard her feet padding against the floor, then she was standing beside him, her old homemade white sacking gown swishing about her knees, and looking down, she exclaimed, "Lordy-mercy-me!"

She knelt and looked at the baby, moving the brown paper off of its little chest. "Why, what beast could of done this!" she cried. "Look at its cold little hands, Jack!"

"Waaaaaaaaaaaah! Waaaaaaaaaaaaaah! Waaaaaa-aaaaaah!"

"Nnnnnnnow, thennnnnnnnnnn!" Mama O'Neal crooned, picking it up and swaying it in her arms.

"Let me hold it! Let me hold it!" Peggy Jo begged.

"Not now, sugar!" Mama O'Neal answered. "It's so tiny, you know . . . ain't even been bathed since gitting borned."

"I'll put on the kettle!" Peggy Jo cried.

"Yeah. And Jack, hit looks like you're gonna have to go in to town as soon as daylight comes and buy some bottles."

"If we just had Nanny Bell back!" Peggy Jo cried, running back toward the kitchen nook.

"What's this?" Jack said, holding up a sheet of paper stuck to the baby's bottom. "Why it's a note of some kind!"

Morning, neighbors,
My name is Camden Jones, on account of I was born in Camden, Arkansas, at three o'clock this morning. My parents ain't got a nickel, so won't you please take me in? My parents seen your dog. We ain't as sorry as you think we are. We know folks who keep dogs ain't going to be mean to a little baby, so please give me a home! My mother's heart is broken, but she's going way, way off—clean to the East Coast. Please.

"Oh, God!" Mama O'Neal squalled as she read the note. "Oh, God! Oh, God . . . dear blessed Saviour!"

"Mama! Git aholt of yourself!" Jack called.

He blinked back hot tears from his eyes, but Mama O'Neal couldn't control herself. "Oh, God! Oh, dear Holy Father!"

179

Jack made a rush for the door, and as he plunged out into the gray darkness, he let go and cried into the soft wind coming off the Mississippi River.

He stood there a long time in the darkness, watching the pink fingers of the sun crawl up the sky. Inside, he heard the baby crying again—heard Mama O'Neal's crooning voice, her big feet padding against the pine-plank flooring, then the rattle of pots and pans, and the hissing kettle.

A bread truck droned past the barracks, but he was not aware of it. The baby, no doubt born in the back seat of an old fifth-hand car, had touched him. Why? Why?

It seemed like a vision that he had. He saw the great highways of America, and the endless line of traffic, bumper to bumper. Restless Americans! Eating their white bread too fast! Slaves to four-thousand-dollar autos, twenty-thousand-dollar houses, and to the monster, one-eyed and terrible, who lurked in the living room, making them live faster, faster, faster—eating up themselves.

Where had the parents been going? What hidden hunger drove them?

How can man-woman, the creators of life, so readily destroy themselves, and even their own creation?

Chapter 14

"Where in the world is yo' ma and Peggy Jo?" Mr. Ferguson asked.

The sun was just then pushing over the levee. More than fifty pickers were in the field, silently pulling the dew-damp locks, and though it was yet cool, dreading the wet heat that would hover over them once the sun had climbed above the levee.

"Mama and Peggy Jo is to home this morning," Jack answered.

"Yeah. I figured that, but why? Are they sick are sompin'?"

"Nope, not sick."

"What's wrong with you, boy? Why are you so moody this morning?"

Mr. Ferguson was peering intently at Jack, one hand slowly transferring a ball of cotton into the long, dragging sack.

"Nothing."

Jack didn't know if he should tell Mr. Ferguson about the baby, because Mama O'Neal didn't know if she would keep it or not. It seemed, she had said, that it was hard enough on Jack, for him having to see to her and Peggy Jo, much less take on a baby, who'd require formula powder, new bottles, more and more nipples as he got old enough to bite the tops out of them, besides all of the rash of childhood diseases he'd surely have, and the resultant drug and medical bills.

"Jack, blame your hide! Don't you be holding nothing back from me, boy!" Mr. Ferguson said angrily. "Now, I been with you through storm and sun and good times and bad! An-ser, I know sompin's wrong. What was all that tarryhooting around down there this morning? And—didn't I see your old truck leave out afore breakfast heading for town?"

"Can you keep a secret?" Jack asked.

"Can I keep a secret! Why, I keep secrets the way a miser keeps money!"

Jack told him about the baby. "It touched me," Jack said, when he'd finished. "And I don't know why."

"Best thing to do is turn hit in to the welfare," Mr. Ferguson advised. "Why, hit's hard enough for grown folks to fiddlefoot around, much less young'uns! Why, I reckon them little Mexican young'uns is rightly the onliest ones who could stand hit!"

"It may sound crazy, but it seems like the baby was sent to me for a purpose," Jack returned. "Mama and Peggy Jo feel the same way I do, too."

"But—God Almighty, son! That little rascal will drink a cow dry of milk!"

Jack looked at the old Texan. Was there a secret fear in his eyes? That Jack might leave him to go on the road alone?

Jack knew that self-preservation is the strongest of all drives, and Jack was already having to pick the high branches of the peach trees. There would come a day when he'd have to carry the old fellow's hamper to the next tree, for his "rheumitiz" had acted up on him during the rainy stay in Missouri.

"I know the baby means trouble, still it came to us so mysteriously," Jack said, doggedly.

"Well, I reckon hit do look right mysterious," Mr. Ferguson returned. "But I'm a-thinking what hit'll do to you, son. Take your mama, she ain't in the field this morning, nor Peggy Jo, and if you keep that young'un, one of them will have to stay with hit every single day!"

"Yeah, and I do have that big debt hanging over my head," Jack agreed.

"Right."

Mama O'Neal didn't come back to the field until the next day. She picked until noon, then spent the afternoon with the baby and let Peggy Jo pick. Right off, Peggy Jo let Jack know that she'd rather stay in with the baby than pick.

"Mama would have let me, too, but he came down with the colic, and boy, did he bawl!" Peggy Jo said.

"Another trip to town for a different formula," Jack smiled.

Somehow, he didn't mind waiting on the wrinkled, writhing little thing. Last night, he'd hung out a foottubload of diapers for it on the back fence, and hadn't minded getting up for the two o'clock feeding to help Mama O'Neal.

A week passed. The last money order Jack had sent the Colonel had been for three dollars, all he had extra. A few days later, Jack got a letter from Colonel House's daughter who lived in town. Briefly, she stated that her father had had a stroke, but that he was doing fine presently, and the old man didn't want Jack to go hungry just to pay him off.

Two days after he got the letter from Colonel House's daughter, the welfare woman came out to the barracks and inquired around about the baby. The four Mexican families told her right off that they didn't know anything about a baby coming mysteriously to the O'Neal's. But a family of Americans, an old couple who drank beer and fussed a lot in such loud voices that the whole barracks heard them, mentioned that they'd heard it crying.

Mr. Ferguson had overheard the conversation. He had been sitting out on the grass reading yesterday's newspaper, and he came to the O'Neal's apartment as soon as she had driven off down the dusty road.

"I was afraid this was going to happen," he said to Jack. "The best thing you can do is go to town and turn hit in, pore little orphan biddy that hit is!"

"No, sir!" Jack said, angrily. "She's not going to git him! Nobody is!"

He was jerking with anger—an anger that came so suddenly that he didn't understand it.

"Well, what you gonna do?" the old Texan growled. "Hit's against the law to keep hit, I think!"

"We're leaving here tonight!" Jack breathed.

"But we ain't been paid for today's picking!" Mr. Ferguson said.

"We're leaving tonight! What's three or four dollars?"

Suddenly Jack was running toward the door. "Mama!" he called. "Mama!"

She met him at the door, the baby cradled in one great, muscular arm. "What is it, son?" she asked.

He told her quickly, and when he'd finished, she ran to a window overlooking the backyard and called, "Peggy Jo! Peggy Jo, young'un, hurry up and come in out'n that heat!"

In a moment Peggy Jo, her face flushed and with beads of sweat glistening on her forehead, came in at the back.

"What's wrong, Mama?" she asked.

Mama told her, speaking in a slow, halting manner like she did when she was worried about something. Peggy Jo patiently listened, but toward the end, a frown creased her pale forehead.

185

"Now, see there!" Peggy Jo said, shrilly. "If you just had a husband, *they* wouldn't bother our baby!"

"Ah, foot, girl!" Mama O'Neal returned, her face reddening. "I've had my bait of being married!"

"Mama, why don't you marry Tex?" Peggy Jo giggled. "Then he could stay in the house with us all the time!"

"That old man!"

"He ain't all that old, Mama! I mean, he can still get around good . . . well, pretty good, and you know how crazy he is over Jack."

"You'd better say you!" Mrs. O'Neal snorted. "Who is it he's always buying Cokes for? And ice cream, and dolls?"

"Yeah!" Peggy Jo grinned. "I think you two would make a good match!"

"Shut that up girl! Git in there and git to packing!"

This was not the first time that Peggy Jo had mentioned marriage to her mother, Jack remembered. And when Mr. Ferguson came over to eat with the family, Peggy Jo always managed to seat him close to her mother.

Jack eyed Mr. Ferguson who yet stood at the front of the barracks. He seemed to be watching the bull bats soaring high above the camp, for his head turned, leveled, as one zoomed down, its stiffened wings making a sound like a German World War Two dive bomber, the kind Jack had seen in movies.

The old man stood there a bit longer, looking, listening. Crickets fiddled in the high hogweeds along the shoulders of the highway. A hazy cloud rode high up in the sad, late October sky. Then Mr. Ferguson began singing "Sanantone Rose," throwing his head back so that the words came out clear and beautiful, as he walked stiffly toward his apartment.

Chapter 15

They fled westward, the speedometer sometimes quivering around the fifty mark, as Jack gunned the old truck downhill, wide open. In the cracked outside mirror, he could see Mr. Ferguson's old horny face leaning outside the window of the flivver. He threw up one balled fist, yelled inaudible words to Jack. Jack knew that he wanted him to slow the truck down. Instead, he pressed the accelerator to the floorboard, until the ancient rattletrap quivered like the back and flanks of a horse trying to shake off a horsefly.

At last, when Jack was forced to pull in at a filling station sitting on a green concrete island, on the left side of the road, Mr. Ferguson pulled alongside in the flivver, its radiator steaming and gurgling, and bawled, "What in the devil is the hurry?"

"Fleeing with my household!" Jack yelled above the roar of the truck's motor. "Just like Moses did from the Pharaoh!"

The gas station attendant motioned for Jack to pull the truck up some. He was in uniform. He wore glasses, and a smile as phony as a nine-dollar bill.

"Fill-er-up," Jack told him.

"What about your oil?"

"Put me in two quarts of forty-weight Havoline, please."

"Shoooop!" the man let out. "This old crate must drink that oil!"

"Yeah, I have to stop more often for oil than for gas."

"I want a Coke," Peggy Jo said, timidly.

"Sure," Jack smiled, reaching one hand into a front pocket for a dime.

He felt extremely happy for some reason. For one thing, the baby was sleeping comfortably on Mama O'Neal's ample lap; for another, he'd put well over two hundred miles between the baby and the welfare woman! The Texas line was up ahead, no more than fifty miles.

East Texas, Jack found, was just like north Louisiana and south Arkansas, with rolling hills, deep pine forests, and a lot of little shirttail farms, mostly set out with pine seedlings, else with fat cattle grazing on the faraway slopes.

In their run to the west, in a small town twenty-eight miles east of Dallas, they stopped for two days to gather pecans for a widow woman named Katy Meyers, in order to pick up some quick money. The trees were old, very tall. Jack had to climb them, then use a long fishing pole to knock down the nuts in the very top branches. Since the pecan orchard was deeply shaded, Mama O'Neal placed Camden Jones in a tuna-fish crate near where she was picking up the thin-shelled nuts, and kept the flies and gnats shooed off with a pasteboard fan with a Garret Snuff advertisement on the back of it. The days were fairly cool, the picking was good, and when Katy Meyers paid Jack off, his check was for fifty-one dollars, the easiest money he'd ever made.

"Why don't we just stay here?" Mama O'Neal asked, the morning they packed up and got ready to pull out.

"Naw, naw! There's a widder womern waiting fer me in Hobbs, New Mexico," Mr. Ferguson boomed. "By this time, I reckon all them young'uns of her'n have married off."

"Why, you old coot! Ain't no woman would marry you!" Mama O'Neal teased.

"Wait and see! Just wait and see!" he mouthed.

. . . From Fort Worth on, Texas was an affront. Like the smells of a hospital! Lean cattle walked lazily through thickets of mesquite. Grassy plains gave way to sand and rock with barb wire separating the ranches. There were yet windmills about, some pointed motionless at the way the wind was last blowing; some spinning rapidly, pumping up the hard, alkaline water for the spotted horses to bury their pink muzzles in. There were hundreds of heat-whipped, dust-covered towns and villages, each with its parcel of sitters and chaw-tobaccos at courthouse and post office. Sometimes, a Mexican wagon would pull up at a hitching post down a wide street, and the mules would stand drowsily, with their heads down, while the hombre shopped for cornmeal, coffee, and lard.

At last their mad run to the west ended at the sprawling Lazy Y Ranch, sixteen miles west of Snyder, Texas. There were shacks for the pickers. Jack learned that first night that the cracks in the wall let in the dust, but also let it out. A cold front had tried to move in from the north, but the rain petered out before it reached the ranch. Later, the winds got up to forty miles per hour, roiling up clouds of brown dust that pinked against the four-eyed window of the shack like sleet. Mama O'Neal protected Camden's face and nose with a blanket, and while the winds howled and shrieked and shook the little shack until the pot-gut heater danced on the pine-plank floor, the baby slept peacefully.

The winds died down during the night, long after Jack had gone off to sleep. He awakened at four o'clock that morning. From the faraway hills came the forlorn whistle of a sheepherder, then his lost, lonely cry to his dog: "Here, Rhody! Here! Here! Here!"

When he heard the sheepherder's whistle and cry no more, he became conscious of the distant, monotonous dub-dub-dub of oil field pumps. He hadn't

noticed the derricks when they had come through
last night. In east Texas, Lord! The oil derricks sat
solidly side by side, like a picket fence, especially
around Longview.

Not until he'd eaten breakfast and had gone outside, did Jack notice the coolness of the air. He came
back in and spoke to Mama O'Neal. "Better stay in
this morning. Wind's cold as deep well water!"

Peggy Jo had shaken the grit out of her jeans; had
stood around sneezing while she tried to balance herself and put them on.

"I don't like old Texas!" she whimpered.

"Well, shut up, and don't whine!" Mama O'Neal
bawled.

"I want to go back to Arkansas, or Mississippi, or
North Carolina, or Missouri, or *anywhere* else but
here!" she sniffed.

"I don't like it much, either," Mama O'Neal said,
"but at least baby is safe here."

"Won't nobody come out here, this far, to get him,
not even God!" Peggy Jo sniffed.

In the cotton field, Mr. Ferguson was jolly most of
the morning despite the cold, which had turned his
big hands to the color of huckleberries. The cotton
had made an excellent crop. The ranch had several
deep wells for irrigation, and besides that, heavy
snows the past winter had soaked the land with moisture. The pay was three dollars per hundred, on the
few ranches and farms where the owners yet preferred human to mechanical pickers.

But Mr. Ferguson didn't like the oil field pumps, nor the steel derricks rising up on the high plains, nor the refinery twelve miles southwest of Snyder, now owned and operated by Monsanto Chemical. He didn't like the way the Mexicans spoke the English language better than he did; nor the way they seemed to think they were as "good" as he was.

"Hit's all changed!" he said, in a mournful voice. "Hit ain't right for a man to come home, and hit not look like home ort to!"

"You're just getting old, Mr. Ferguson," Mama said in a bantering voice.

"I ain't as young as I used to be, no. But I know blamed well hit didn't use to git this cold here in the first week of November! Why, I recollect that I kilt a sidewinder oncet on Thanksgiving Day. Hit was sunning hitself on a rock, and I think I was walking barefooted."

"What's a sidewinder?" Peggy Jo wanted to know.

"Hit's a rattlesnake, gal," Mr. Ferguson said. "I bet you there's more rattlesnakes in them draws and gulchs than there are people living up to town!"

Mr. Ferguson drove into Snyder after work that evening and came back in a black mood. He was living in the shack just across a narrow irrigation ditch from the one the O'Neals occupied. For a long time that night, in spite of the cold, he stood out in the yard and whittled on a piece of mesquite bush, and talked to Jack.

"I rode all over town and didn't see hair nor hide of anybody I know," he said sadly. "And there wasn't a horse nor wagon in town! Not a single blacksmith shop that I saw, either!"

"I reckon the baby has done something to me," Jack answered. "Somehow, I ain't eager to hit the road like I was."

"Hit was the way the baby come to you folks, and all," Mr. Ferguson mused. "But I say, once a fiddle-foot, always a fiddlefoot. Now, if you'd latched on to that little Tommy . . ."

"She ain't for me," Jack said quickly.

"She's gonna be a looker when she grows up, fer a fact," the old man smiled.

"Yeah, but she was a town girl—we just don't have nothing in common."

"If this cold snap hadn't come on, I might have drove in to Hobbs, New Mexico," Mr. Ferguson mused. "I like to have hitched up with a widder wom-ern there oncet, but ain't no telling—the way every-thing has changed around here, she may be done dead and buried."

"I know a widow woman lots closer to you than old Hobbs, New Mexico!" came Peggy Jo's piping voice. She was standing in the door, a grin on her lips.

"Go way from here, gal!" Mr. Ferguson boomed. "First thing you know, and I'll put some wood agin your sitter!"

"Well, if you're really wanting to marry . . ."

"Peggy Jo, git in this house!" Mama O'Neal yelled from the kitchen.

Mr. Ferguson shook his fist at Peggy Jo as she went in, but he was grinning. "You consarned little vixen!" he holloed.

But Jack noted that the old man liked for Peggy Jo to tease him about Mama O'Neal, and lately he was always ready to fetch her wood for the heater, or a bucket of water from the pump, or a spool of thread from town, and it seemed to Jack that he'd sit and watch her much more than he used to.

"Mr. Ferguson, I've been doing some thinking," Jack said. "When spring comes, I may go back to see Colonel House. He propositioned me with a land offer. The baby ought to have a better chance than I did, and Peggy Jo is still young enough to finish high school. She can start back in the fifth grade—if she'll start."

"Jack O'Neal, you know you'll never be happy agin unless you're on the road!" Mr. Ferguson said. "Now, cut out that foolishness! Let that baby see to hitself. Hit ain't nothing but a maverick, nohow!"

Two weeks later, a howling blizzard blew in from New Mexico, depositing the driest six inches of snow on the flat land that Jack had ever seen before. This was the final blow. Mr. Ferguson raved for an hour about the cold and the way the feathery snow seeped through the cracks in the plank shacks, as he stood cold and miserable behind the potbellied stove. Mama

O'Neal had tucked in the baby. He lay on the bed, his blue eyes moving around some when he heard the unfamiliar voice.

"Goo! Coooooo!" he said.

The coos thrilled Mama O'Neal so, she reared back and laughed until tears came in her eyes.

Peggy Jo came running. "I heard him!" she cried. And then, touching the baby's fine, blue-black hair, "Gootchy gootchy gootchy! Do it again!"

Jack crossed to the foot of the bed, and stood there looking at the "little rascal." What a mystery! How could anything grow so fast! All of the wrinkles on face, body, hands and feet were gone now, and he was red only when he cried.

"Jack, ain't he purty, though!" Mama said.

"Yeah, he is," Jack answered.

"Huh! The way you folks take on over that brat is enough to make a feller urp!" Mr. Ferguson scoffed.

"Ah, Tex"—Peggy Jo had taken to calling him that —"you're just jealous!" Peggy Jo needled.

"You'll think jealous when that little maverick comes down with the six-month colic and you have to walk him all night long!" Mr. Ferguson snorted.

Later that morning, the wind died, and it seemed to Jack, as he stood by the window, that the little shack was set down in a great silence. Jackrabbits came out of the draws and mesquite thickets and hopped soundlessly in the great white silence.

Roosevelt, the hackles standing up on the back of his neck like saw teeth, came rushing out of his lair underneath the shack and gave chase, and Jack watched dog and rabbits disappear in the mesquite.

"Reckon how picking will be after the thaw?" Jack asked.

"No good a-tall," Mr. Ferguson answered. "But hit didn't use to snow before Christmas out here. Blamed if I know what's got wrong with the weather!"

That afternoon, when the sun came out, a friend of Mr. Ferguson's rode up to the O'Neal shack on a burro. He had a chicken crate balanced in front of the small saddle, with a number of yellow fryers inside it.

"Hello, señor!" he called. "Hello!"

Jack opened the door to him. "Get down and come in," Jack invited.

In his dealings with the Mexicans Jack had found them easygoing, quiet, unless they had beer; pleasant if they didn't have too much of it.

"No, no, señor!" the old Mexican said. "The weather, she's cold. So I sell my chik-on! I have lovely chik-ons! See!"

Friendly brown eyes, with something sad about them, too, peered at Jack over a quivering handlebar moustache.

"How much do you want apiece for them?" Jack asked.

Thin lips peeled back in a sad smile, revealing a line of white teeth set like a keyboard in a brown piano.

"Oh, señor! I could not price theem!" he said, waving his hands gracefully.

"Why not?"

"Oh, señor, because these are the sons and daughters of my heart!"—he was pointing at the crate. "Thees wan ees Manuel. He has the rich comb, señor! And thees wan is Manuela. She is so dainty when she drinks at the well, señor! And thees wan ees Pedrito. Oh, he has a temper! And thees wan ees little Susita! *Pobre pequeno pollito!*"

For a moment, Jack thought that the old man was crying. His hands reached through the slats in the crate and stroked the yellow feathers, until the fryers began to squawk.

"I'll give fifty cents for one," Jack offered.

"Ah, señor! Which wan?"

"I'll buy Manuela."

"Ah, but not for fifty cents, señor! Manuela is the daughter of my heart!"

"Seventy-five cents."

"Ah, señor! That ees more like eet!"

He busied himself with opening up the crate, while Jack searched his pockets until he found three quarters.

"Poor little cup of gold!" the old man crooned, bringing the dubious-eyed pullet out of the crate, then stroking her yellow feathers. "But better thees than the filthy stench of Hosea Gomez's market!"

He handed the trembling bird to Jack. It felt warm in Jack's hands. Its heart beat very fast.

"Good-bye, little daughter of my heart!" the old man sighed. "But the days grow cold and my feed is short. Better thees than Gomez's filthy market."

Jack waited until the old Mexican had coaxed the burro in a high, whining voice; until he finally moved, his pointed hoofs clopping in the feathery snow. Then he carried his prize in for Mama O'Neal's inspection.

"Lord, don't bring that chicken into my kitchen!" she said, throwing up both hands and shaking her head.

"She's pretty fat," Jack returned.

"Yeah, but I'd choke on her gizzard after hearing the way that old man took on so! Why, he called hit his daughter! You can wring hits neck, scald, pick, and dress hit if you want to, but I ain't touching hit! You hear me, Jack O'Neal!"

"Yes'm."

"Wring its neck, Jack! Scald, pick and clean it! I'll eat it!" Peggy Jo announced.

Mama O'Neal gave her daughter a scornful look. "You hardhearted thing!" she shamed her.

"Well, if we don't eat it, somebody will!" Peggy Jo answered. "Any way you take it, that pullet never did have a chance."

Mama O'Neal looked out at the cold, silent plains. "I sometimes think a *body* is just like a chicken," she said, with a melancholy twist to her voice. "A body gits borned and is shoved out of the nest, and if a body is lucky he escapes from the fox and snake, but his fate is sealed. He ends up at Gomez's filthy market, or what is about as bad, some rich feller's ranch."

200

Jack knew she was in one of her infrequent dark moods. Money was scarce, food short, winter coming on, and no big order of heavy jackets and thick socks sent out to Sears Roebuck yet.

"Mama, we gonna make it!" Jack said, stoutly. "Mama, when spring comes, maybe we can go back to the Delta, buy a little land and—"

"It takes money to buy land!" she cut in.

"Maybe I can get a steady job then, and we can settle down on a little farm and keep a cow, fifteen hens, and a pig to eat the slop."

"It sounds good, but I ain't got much hope about settling down no more," she sighed. And then, looking out the window, her eyes seeing vistas of another time, "Once, I begged your pa to settle down, Jack. My mouth watered for some land that I could call mine. But he had itchy feet. He wouldn't listen, and now it don't matter no more."

"But, Mama, I see change everywhere," he said quietly. "The mechanical picker has replaced man, you might say. As soon as these old folks die who own the plantations and farms, you won't see people like us in the fields no more."

"Them inventors ain't made no machine that can pick peaches and apples and tomatoes," she answered.

"Yeah, but in time they will! Some are already trying new things. Mr. Ferguson showed me a piece in the paper last month where one orchard man was using a blower to gather the apples. It's some kind of wind-making machine. It just blows the apples off, like a hurricane does, you know."

201

"Foot, Jack! Do you expect me to believe every crackpot thing a body sees in them old murder and violence sheets?"

"Just the same, I've been thinking, Mama. I guess the baby done it, the way he come to us, so mysterious and all, is what done it!" he said.

She turned and looked quickly at the snug bundle on the low bed. "Ain't he the cutest thing, though!" she smiled.

"Well, that's what I'm getting at, Mama! We've got to make a choice between him and the road!"

She looked at him a long time, then sadly shook her head. "Son, fiddlefoots don't have no choice," she said.

Chapter 16

The cold spell held on for a week. The cotton fields hadn't thawed. All of Jack's money was gone. Mr. Ferguson came and squatted by the potbellied stove and bemoaned their luck.

"I ain't never coming back to Texas, if the good Lord will just let me make enough money to leave hit!" he said. "It didn't use to be this way, though. Why, I can remember walking through them draws barefooted on Thanksgiving Day many a time!"

But the cold held on. Jack's family knew want, hunger and fear. Camden Jones first came down with the earache. Jack chopped up a load of the mesquite bushes and fed the faggots into the red-hot maw of the heater, and Mama O'Neal poured out the last of the salt from the five-pound sack into a black skillet, heated it on the cookstove, then poured it into a tobacco sack and held it to the baby's inflamed ear until he got relief. Then Peggy Jo came down with the Asian flu, ran a high fever for two days, during which time she was out of her head, and talked like a

Holiness preacher. Two days later, Camden took it. He was so sick he didn't even cry, but lay on the bed in a frightening stupor. Jack drove into Snyder and begged Doctor Alvarez to come out and treat the baby.

Doctor Alvarez was a kindly, dark, young Spanish American. But the money squeeze had caught him, and he even refused to treat his own people unless they put up money or stock (cows, pigs, goats) in advance. A seventy-thousand-dollar house out in the fashionable new addition west of town, a stable of fine, gaited horses that he kept on a small ranch he'd bought, and a wife who vacationed in Mexico City each year during the bullfight season were enough to harden his heart.

But Jack pressed him. "I'll do anything! Just any kind of work you got, if only you'll doctor the baby!" he promised.

"What about cleaning stables?"

"Gladly."

Dr. Alvarez called on the baby in the shack west of Snyder, and Jack called on the fine ranch barn about eight miles south of that city down toward Big Springs, and forked up manure for three days to pay for the doctor's visit.

Two days later, with his little body chock-full of antibiotics and antiviruses, Camden began to coo again.

But the cold weather held on, and the cotton hung limply from the burrs, now blackened and rotting in the fields. Each day, Mr. Ferguson became more restless. "By Ganny, I'd even consider gitting on the old age, if hit would help git me off of these here high plains!" he said one day as he squatted beside the heater.

"Pinto beans for breakfast, pinto beans for lunch, and pinto beans for supper!" Mama O'Neal snapped.

"And the ones you git around here has got rocks in them," Mr. Ferguson fussed. "I chomped down on a bite this morning and nearly broke out my two good jaw teeth on a rock as big as a hunk of coal!"

The next day, Jack drove into town and applied for work at the employment office, which was located in the old post office building near the bank.

A balding, bespecked man peered at Jack for a moment. He must have seen the hunger in his eyes. "How old are you, son?"

"Eighteen," Jack said, which was a whopping lie.

"Yeah?" And then, "You ever clean out oil tanks?"

"No, sir."

"It's hard work."

"I don't mind that."

"All right. Report to Mr. Sniderman out at the Gulf Camp and if you don't know where it's at, ask someone."

Jack found the camp, located Mr. Sniderman, and went to work. Two helpers let him down into the huge, empty metal tank where he shoveled sludge into lifts for five hours. He went home that night black, soaked with oil.

"Lordy-mercy-me! What kind of thing did you fall into, Jack?" Mama O'Neal asked.

Jack saw Peggy Jo staring at him. "I got desperate, and so I just took me a pick and shovel and dug me an oil well," he grinned.

"Mama, ain't he lying!" she snapped.

For four days' work, Jack received two hundred and nineteen dollars. All of the sludge was cleaned out of the tanks. There wouldn't be any more work for several days, so the little family hit the road again, heading east. "Sompin' tells me while we got the money to git, we better git!" he told Mama O'Neal.

For two weeks, they worked their way across Texas. Mostly, it was Jack doing the work. In Dallas he took a job with a carnival outfit. He helped set up crack-the-whips, merry-go-rounds, Ferris wheels.

The afternoon his job ended, Jack was standing near a cotton candy booth, listening to the sad nostalgia of the music the merry-go-round made, when he looked up and saw Irish O'Bannion walking out from behind the line of tents. She didn't see him, so he called, "Hey, Irish!"

She stopped dead still, turned and looked for him.

He stepped away from the cotton candy booth. "Over here," he said, then walked toward her.

"Jack!" she yelled. She came running, sprang into his arms, hugged him tight.

"Imagine seeing you in a place like this!" he breathed.

She was standing close. He caught the clean-girl fumes of her. But she had on tawdry slacks, a cheap, sleazy blouse, and her hair looked burnt or something.

"Yeah, we've been with this outfit for six weeks now," Irish said sadly.

"What happened?"

"A lot of things. Mother couldn't find any kind of job, Jack, and school was like you said it would be."

"They snubbed you, then!"

"Some did, even in that poor make-out-of-a-town!"

Jack bought pink and red cotton candy for both of them, and they walked through the carnival grounds, and made light talk—as light, ethereal as the sugary goo they nibbled at—until it was time for Irish to get ready for the big opening that night. She sold tickets for a sideshow featuring six headhunters from the Amazon. "Really, they came off an Indian Reservation in Arizona," she giggled.

Her mother worked in a food booth. She was downtown shopping for some new nylons, so Jack didn't get to see her.

They held hands for a long time at the main gate, and Jack finally said, "If I ever settle down, maybe I can see you again, Irish."

There was a sad look in her eyes. "That won't never be," she said, softly. "Besides, I don't know where you'd find me. I don't even know how long we'll stay with this outfit."

Quickly, he told her about Camden, and how the baby had changed up his itchy mind.

"You folks better adopt him!" she warned. "You'll raise him up to a good big young'un, and his parents will come and get him."

"I've thought about that, but you know as good as I do that the welfare folks won't let us adopt Camden until we settle down and buy him a home."

"Irish O'Bannion!" a hoarse voice called. "Irish!"

"That's old man Wyatt!" she said angrily. "Watches me like a hawk! I'm supposed to be helping with the sideshow stuff. Bye, Jack."

"Bye, Irish!"

Chapter 17

It was the first week in December when they drew
near Lake Providence. The Delta lay dormant under
cold, gray winter clouds. The cotton fields were blackened. Water stood ankle deep in the low places, for
it had been a rainy November. Frogs glee-anked,
glee-anked, glee-anked in the marshes along the
levee. At times, Jack glimpsed the sad, glorious sweep
of the mighty Mississippi snaking toward the Gulf of
Mexico.

He recalled things he thought he'd forgotten. A
flight of ducks got up from a marsh where they'd been
feeding on wild rice and stuttered off in a wild flight
for safety, crossing the highway in front of the old
truck. He remembered a frost-rimmed swamp out
from Truxno where he and his father had lain in wait
for a big, fat gander; a day in April when he'd walked
barefoot across Colonel House's pasture, his feet as
tender as violet heads, in his mad rush to catch up
with his dad, who was high-tailing it to the lake, fishing tackle in one hand.

Now, there was a cold, winter grave in old Truxno Graveyard, in the way of the deer trails. There would be shy hoofprints in the cold Delta ground, with the little headpiece that marked Wesley O'Neal's resting place.

As they drew near Colonel House's plantation, Jack thought of other things, too. He thought of Rita Alvarez, and the way she'd sit there in the tent, and outside the tent, and read the history and civics books; and the time she read aloud to him in a soft, silibant singsong:

"We hold these truths to be self-evident: that all men are created equal; that they are endowed by their Creator with certain unalienable Rights; that among these are Life, Liberty, and the pursuit of Happiness . . ."

Ahead of them lay the antebellum mansion behind a forest of pecan trees, its great pillars cold and white under the melancholy winter clouds. He wondered if he'd have the courage to face Colonel House, and tell him he'd have to wait on more money for a spell. He wondered if he could make himself ask the Colonel if he would still consider letting Jack settle down on some of his land, like he did Jack's father.

Jack had talked it over with his mother. "Our only chance to adopt Camden is to settle down," he said. "If you're willing to risk it."

She had snugged the baby tight against her ample breasts. "It's the same as if he was my own now," she said. "Yes, I'll risk it."

The colored maid welcomed Jack with a smile, but there was something sad about it, too. "Come in."

"Who is it?" came the low-pitched, cultured voice of a woman.

"A boy come to see C'unl House lak he allus do!" the maid answered.

"Show him in."

A richly dressed woman with eyes that reminded Jack of the Colonel's entered the living room from the hall at the same time he came in at the door. Her face was rather pretty, rather sad, and yet there was something warm and homey about it, too.

"I—I've come to see the Colonel," Jack mumbled, his cap in one hand.

Her face altered. The smile changed to a quivery movement of her lips, like she was about to cry.

"Haven't you heard?" she asked.

"Heard what, ma'am?"

"Dad died last November, the day after Thanksgiving."

Jack felt a sinking sensation at the pit of his stomach. His head reeled. All in one moment, he knew that his plans, hopes, were fruitless. But he remembered to be polite.

"No'm. I ain't heard about him," Jack answered. "I'm really sorry, ma'am. He was a good man."

"Yes, Dad was!" And she began to smile again. "You know, your words lifted, consoled me. What bigger tribute could be paid him than to hear it from a—"

"Fiddlefoot," he finished for her.

"Well, frankly—I mean, Dad knew and dealt with all kinds of people, but he always told me while I was growing up that the migrants were good, kind people who'd had bad luck, or in some cases, had itchy feet. Anyway, he trusted them."

"Ma'am, I've come here to see about a debt," Jack said.

"Well, you'll have to go up to Lake Providence and see Harvey Fielding. He's been Dad's lawyer for forty years, I think. He's finishing up with the will, and I believe that Dad left a letter for you."

"A letter?"

"Yes, I think so."

Jack thanked her and left. Wonder what in the world could be in that letter? he thought. Probably something about the loan. It didn't matter. Nothing mattered. There was a taste of spoiled peanuts in his mouth, and to make things worse, when he came up to the truck, Camden was bawling to the top of his lungs.

"Did you see him?" Mama O'Neal asked, as he got into the truck.

"He's dead. It's all over. We just as well hit the road again."

"Where to now?" Mr. Ferguson bawled, his head out the window of the flivver.

"Going on up to Lake Providence. From there, I couldn't say," Jack yelled.

"You lead, and I'll follow!" the old Texan called.

Jack parked the ancient vehicle in the alley behind the courthouse, because he was afraid to risk leaving it at the front, from fear of the State Police. For one thing, he needed a taillight, and the brakes had to be pumped four or five times before they would hold. Then, if the State Troopers caught him, and wanted to be snotty, they could stick him for driving with the burst muffler.

He entered the courthouse through the back entrance. A colored janitor with a push broom in one hand showed him the door of Harvey Fielding's office. It was warm in the long, wide corridor, for the courthouse was a new one with central heating, and Jack didn't smell the old familiar scents of musty courtrooms, splattered cuspidors, and funky basements.

He stood at the door and read the brass lettering: HARVEY FIELDING, ATTORNEY AT LAW, knocked, and heard the peck-peck of spike heels.

The door opened, and a smiling middle-aged woman dressed in a trim brown coat-suit invited him in. He told her whom he wanted to see.

"In there," she pointed. "Harvey will see you now."

Jack entered Harvey Fielding's inner sanctum and stood in front of his desk without being seen for a moment. The old lawyer was reared back in the swivel chair, his eyes closed. On the wall, hanging on a peg, was his gray jacket and gray Western hat.

Jack cleared his throat and was suddenly looking into dark brown, red-rimmed eyes. "Yes?" the lawyer said, thickly.

"I come to see about a letter from the Colonel his daughter says you're holding for me," Jack answered.

"Oh? Sure, sure!"

The old lawyer came stiffly to his feet, and as he crossed to a metal filing cabinet, Jack saw that he had a beer-keg belly, though that was the only place where he looked fat. His face was a warm pink from the heat, quite handsome in a dignified way, and a mane of white hair arose from his massive forehead, which gave him a Deep South look.

He came back with a folder, sat down at the desk, which was cluttered with today's newspaper, and maybe last week's letters, and opened the folder up, took out a long, sealed envelope and held it out to Jack.

"You better read it here, I expect," he said. "There is another matter I've got to take up with you before you leave the office."

With trembling hands, Jack opened the envelope up, then brought the crisp, neatly folded sheet out, unfolded it. It was dated July 2, 1964. There was something else folded with it.

214

DEAR JACK:

Enclosed herewith is my check for two hundred and forty-seven dollars, though you haven't paid in near that much. But I lied to you, Jack. Your dad didn't owe me any money. I've torn up the promissory note. You see, I showed you an old note he once gave me to get that old '47 Ford he wrecked up in North Carolina out of the shop. He forgot to pick up the note when he paid me, and I forgot to give it to him later. I thought a heap of your dad, son. And I wanted you to grow up to be a man. I thought about how wild you might go if you had the money to spend for beer and such, so I invented the debt, you might say. I felt guilty for doing it, but I have remembered you in my will. Maybe that will make up for it.

Your friend,
COLONEL R. HOUSE

Jack was aware that Harvey Fielding was eyeing him as he looked at the check, then read the letter over again.

"Boy, I never dreamed of this!" Jack said.

"I suspect you'd like to know what's in the Colonel's will for you, wouldn't you?"

"Yes, sir."

"Well, I can tell you—he left you one hundred acres of that river section. Your land runs right into the Mississippi River bottom."

"Oh, no!" Jack cried.

"Oh, yes!" Harvey Fielding drawled.

"I—I can't believe hit!"

"Well, I'm reading the will officially next Thursday morning at nine o'clock sharp," the lawyer answered.

"You'll see. And did you know, son, that land is selling for fo' hundred dollars an acre—fo' hundred! And back when I was a boy, you could buy it all day long for ten!"

"Thanks, sir! Oh, thanks, thanks!"

"You're welcome . . . see you next Thursday."

Jack was running across the cold wet loam toward the old truck, holding the check in one hand. Mr. Ferguson was standing beside the cab, talking to Mama O'Neal and Peggy Jo and grinning like a mule eating briers, when he saw Jack coming.

"What's the big hurry?" the old Texan drawled, when Jack was there.

"Going home, going home!" Jack sang out.

"Going home where?" Mr. Ferguson's face looked puzzled.

"To my land! My own land!" Jack cried.

Then Jack showed the check, explained all about it, and about how he'd been remembered in the Colonel's will.

"Reckon there'd be enough room for an old fiddlefoot to build a house for his family there?" Mr. Ferguson asked.

"A house for your family? I don't understand," Jack answered, a puzzled look on his face, this time.

"Jack, we're fixing to have a new daddy!" Peggy Jo said, excitedly. "Tex is gonna marry Mama! I heard him ask her, and I heard her say she would!"

"Yep, she shore did," Mr. Ferguson boomed.

216

"In that case, you'd be right welcome," Jack smiled.

"Put her there, podner!" The old man grabbed Jack's hand, pumped it. And then, "I expect I know a little Tommy who'll be welcomed to your land in a few days, too! Send her a telegram, boy!"

Jack smiled broadly, but he did not answer the old Texan, for he was thinking about his words as he slid under the wheel.

About the Author

GEORGE HARMON SMITH was born on a farm, near a swamp, about halfway between Lillie and Spearsville, Louisiana. In addition to working at sawmills, cutting pulpwood, logging, clearing new ground, farming and trapping, he has earned his Bachelor's Degree from Louisiana Tech, his Master's from the University of Arkansas, and an Advanced Master's from the University of Mississippi. In speaking of the latter state, he writes, "I watched William Faulkner's last ride down Lamar Street, and on through Oxford, and saw him buried in the red clay earth he loved so well north of town."

A JOHN DAY BOOK